***Was there any possibility
that he could feel the same way
about her that she did about him?***

Of course not, Tally realized. J. D. Turner was the charter member of the Ain't Getting Married, No Way, Never Club. And if he ever gave up his membership, it wouldn't be for a girl like her.

He leaned toward her and cupped her hand behind her head. She knew she should pull away. She knew that, and yet she greedily wanted every moment he would give her.

Their lips met.

All the control—which she had tried so hard all her life to have—evaporated, just like that. She felt her lips part at his gentle insistence.

His tongue explored the contours of her mouth until they were both panting with wanting, both of them unleashing that which had been so tightly leashed.

Desire.

Passion.

And the scariest

Dear Reader,

If you're like me, you can't get enough heartwarming love stories and real-life fairy tales that end happily ever after. You'll find what you need and so much more with Silhouette Romance each month.

This month you're in for an extra treat. Bestselling author Susan Meier kicks off MARRYING THE BOSS'S DAUGHTER—the brand-new six-book series written exclusively for Silhouette Romance. In this launch title, *Love, Your Secret Admirer* (#1684), our favorite matchmaking heiress helps a naive secretary snare her boss's attention with an eye-catching makeover.

A sexy rancher discovers love and the son he never knew, when he matches wits with a beautiful teacher, in *What a Woman Should Know* (#1685) by Cara Colter. And a not-so plain Jane captures a royal heart, in *To Kiss a Sheik* (#1686) by Teresa Southwick, the second of three titles in her sultry DESERT BRIDES miniseries.

Debrah Morris brings you a love story of two lifetimes, in *When Lightning Strikes Twice* (#1687), the newest paranormal love story in the SOULMATES series. And sparks sizzle between an innocent curator—with a big secret—and the town's new lawman, in *Ransom* (#1688) by Diane Pershing. Will a seamstress's new beau still love her when he learns she is an undercover heiress? Find out in *The Bridal Chronicles* (#1689) by Lissa Manley.

Be my guest and feed your need for tender and lighthearted romance with all six of this month's great new love stories from Silhouette Romance.

Enjoy!

Mavis C. Allen
Associate Senior Editor, Silhouette Romance

Please address questions and book requests to:
Silhouette Reader Service
U.S.: 3010 Walden Ave., P.O. Box 1325, Buffalo, NY 14269
Canadian: P.O. Box 609, Fort Erie, Ont. L2A 5X3

What a Woman Should Know

CARA COLTER

SILHOUETTE *Romance*®

Published by Silhouette Books

America's Publisher of Contemporary Romance

To my delightful nephew,
Chase Craig,
with love

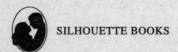

SILHOUETTE BOOKS

ISBN 0-373-19685-7

WHAT A WOMAN SHOULD KNOW

Copyright © 2003 by Cara Colter

This edition published by arrangement with Harlequin Books S.A.

® and TM are trademarks of Harlequin Books S.A., used under license.
Trademarks indicated with ® are registered in the United States Patent
and Trademark Office, the Canadian Trade Marks Office and in other
countries.

Visit Silhouette at www.eHarlequin.com

Printed in U.S.A.

Books by Cara Colter

Silhouette Romance

Dare to Dream #491
Baby in Blue #1161
Husband in Red #1243
The Cowboy, the Baby and the Bride-to-Be #1319
Truly Daddy #1363
A Bride Worth Waiting For #1388
Weddings Do Come True #1406
A Babe in the Woods #1424
A Royal Marriage #1440
First Time, Forever #1464
*Husband by Inheritance #1532
*The Heiress Takes a Husband #1538
*Wed by a Will #1544
What Child Is This? #1585
Her Royal Husband #1600
9 Out of 10 Women Can't Be Wrong #1615
Guess Who's Coming for Christmas? #1632
What a Woman Should Know #1685

*The Wedding Legacy

Silhouette Books

The Coltons
A Hasty Wedding

CARA COLTER

shares ten acres in the wild Kootenay region of British Columbia with the man of her dreams, three children, two horses, a cat with no tail and a golden retriever who answers best to "bad dog." She loves reading, writing and the woods in winter (no bears). She says life's delights include an automatic garage door opener and the skylight over the bed that allows her to see the stars at night.

She also says, "I have not lived a neat and tidy life, and used to envy those who did. Now I see my struggles as having given me a deep appreciation of life, and of love, that I hope I succeed in passing on through the stories that I tell."

J. D. Turner's idea of…

What a Woman Should Know

1) One should not settle for stainless-steel appliances instead of wild nights of passion.

2) Too many rules are damaging to a small boy's spirit, to *anyone's* spirit.

3) Germs are rarely deadly. Dog kisses are one of life's delights.

4) Small boys (and big ones) need to get dirty.

5) Life needs to hold surprises.

6) Women who get married for security end up like dried old prunes who don't laugh enough and are prone to depression in their middle years.

Chapter One

John David Turner loved to sing. The louder the better. He loved to sing until the rafters rang with the sound of his voice, until the walls vibrated around him. He sang when he was happy, and today had been a damned good day, even if he had hurt his shoulder pulling the engine from Clyde Walters's '72 Mustang.

Of course, there was only one place a guy with a singing voice like his—raspy, out-of-key and thunderous—could make noise like that, and that was in the shower. J.D. was indulging himself now.

The hot water pounding down on him, soothing the ache in the shoulder muscle he'd pulled, he belted out his all-time favorite tune. The bathroom was steamy, despite the wide open window, but he had a theory that steam greatly improved acoustics.

"Annabel was a cow of unusual bovine beauty..."

He held the note at the end until it was wrenching, like the song of the coyotes that haunted the shrub and willow-filled gullies west of his place. Sometimes, like now in the early summer, when he finished that final gut-twisting note, drawing out "beaut*eeeeeee*" endlessly, the coyotes even answered him.

So, he paused now to see if that would be the case.

Every window in his small house was open, letting the cool early evening air chase out the unusual heat of the day. His engine repair shop and house sat on the edge of town, just far enough out of Dancer, North Dakota, so that only the coyotes could hear him when he got in one of these I-gotta-sing moods.

But it wasn't the voices of coyotes he heard in the sudden void left by the absence of his voice. He heard a determined knocking on his front door.

He frowned, considering this breach of his privacy. He considered not answering the door. No one knew he sang. No one. Except once, a long time ago, in a moment of pure madness, he had sung a love song.

Don't go there, he told himself.

Though he tried to outwait it, the knocking continued on the front door.

J.D. turned off the shower and grabbed a towel. How could a person go from being so happy, to *this* in the blink of an eye?

Whether he was mad about remembering the love song, or mad because he had been caught singing, or mad because his intruder didn't have the good sense to go away, J.D. was just plain mad as he stomped across his bedroom, towel around his waist, dripping water on his carpets. Who the hell would dare to encroach on his most private moment?

Probably his pal Stan, the town's other bachelor and the only other charter member of the Ain't Gettin' Married, No Way, Never Club—known by its initials A.G.M.N.W.N.C.—who dropped by in the evenings, sometimes, with a couple of beers. They'd spend the evening out in the shop tinkering on some old car. If it was Stan, it would be all over Dancer by tomorrow afternoon that J. D. Turner sang about cows in the shower.

Maybe that wouldn't be big news in most places, but Dancer was a little short on news, big or small. The most inconsequential snippets of private information could tear through the town's eight-block radius like wildfire.

J.D. had the lousy feeling he was going to be listening to cow jokes for a long, long time.

And, of course, if he asked Stan not to say anything, that would only make it worse.

On the other hand, if it was Stan, he could tell him about the progress he'd made on the Mustang today. Would that be enough to wipe serenades to bovines right out of Stan's head? Slightly cheered by the possibility he yanked open the door to his bedroom and marched into the hall.

Expecting Stan, J.D. skidded to a halt in the darkness of his hallway, and stared at the shapely silhouette framed in the last rays from a fading sun that spilled in the round oval screen of his outside front door.

She had turned away from the door, and was looking over the overgrown lilac hedge toward town, hugging herself against the little nip in the prairie breeze. She was wearing a pencil-line skirt that might have looked businesslike, if it hadn't been *her*. On her, that skirt hugged the seductive swell of hip and buttocks, showed off the long, sensuous line of her legs.

Oh yes. Even though her back was to him, he knew who it was.

Her blond hair shimmered in the last of the day's light. It looked like it was in a bun, but some strands had broken free, and the breeze played with them, and they tickled and swayed on the slender column of her neck.

For a moment his mouth went dry, and he remembered the man he had been once, a long, long time ago, when he had sung a woman a love song.

He reminded himself, sharply, he was not that man any longer. He knotted the towel firmly around his waist, and strode down the hall.

Every step increased his fury.

Five years. Not so much as a goodbye. No letter. No phone call. No explanation at all. And then she just reappears in his life?

His plan was to slam the door, and lock it. He'd been bewitched by Elana Smith once and that was more than enough.

And so he was shocked when his fury propelled him past the interior door, right out the screen door, and onto the porch.

He was appalled when his anger spiked, overriding everything in him that was reasonable. He took the slenderness of her shoulder in his hand, and spun her around, and without fully registering the shock on her face, he pulled her hard into him, and kissed her.

It was not a hello kind of kiss.

It was a punishing kiss. Savage. It held the bitter sting of love betrayed, the hurt of five years of asking why. And it held the power of a man who been severely wounded on the battlefield of love, but who had survived, and let those festering wounds make him stronger, harder, colder than he ever had been before.

She was shoving against him, frantically, trying to escape his hold, his lips. He felt momentary satisfaction that her strength was so puny compared to his.

But then it registered, somewhere, peripherally, that

something was wrong. Elana trying to escape his lips? She would have delighted in the savagery. She would have given back as good as she got. She probably would have drawn blood by now.

As he was arriving at these conclusions, he felt the woman surrender beneath the punishing onslaught of his lips. The struggle stopped.

He was contemplating this development, letting the doubt take hold where certainty had been, when she yanked free of him, and belted him up the side of his head with a purse that felt like it had a brick in it.

He staggered back from her and regarded her with narrowed eyes.

He felt as if he'd been hit with more than a brick as he studied the exquisite face that looked back at him.

"How dare you!" she sputtered angrily, glaring at him, and then began wiping away at the front of her blouse, which was wet from his shower-damp skin, as if she could erase his touch from herself.

Oh, it was Elana's face, all right. Heart-shaped, exquisitely feminine, vaguely exotic. How well he remembered those lines—the incredible cheekbones, the pert nose, the faintly pointed chin.

But the *how dare you* in that clipped, tight tone was not Elana. The woman in front of him simply was not Elana.

Underneath the sooty sweep of thick lashes, he realized the eyes were a shade different. Elana's had been blue. These eyes were indigo, like the center of a violet-colored pansy.

Of course, with contact lenses, anything could happen, and he studied the woman more intently.

The anger and fear in her lovely eyes were real. And

right behind them was softness. The same softness he had felt in those lips.

Not, on closer study, Elana's mouth either. Hers had been wide and sensual. This woman's mouth was small, her lips little bows, puffy from being so thoroughly kissed.

He swore under his breath. He'd just kissed the living daylights out of a perfect stranger who had the bad luck to show up as he was remembering that he had once sung a love song. He crossed his arms over his naked chest.

It was obvious to him that she didn't like that he was only wearing a towel. She didn't like it one little bit. She was studying her blouse as though she expected daffodils to bloom from the bosom.

"You've ruined my blouse," she said, finally, her voice stiff with control. "It's silk."

"Yeah. I figured."

She gave him a look that said she didn't think he would know the first thing about silk, so of course he felt prodded to deepen the great first impression he'd made.

"Silk is always see-through when it's wet," he said easily.

Her eyes grew very round. Her mouth formed an indignant *O*. She blushed, and crossed her arms over her breasts, snap, snap, like it was a military maneuver. By-the-numbers, cover chest.

"Too late," he said. "I saw it. Lace trim."

"Oh!" she said.

"Don't hit me with that purse again," he warned her.

"Well, then quit looking at me like that!"

"Like what?"

She sputtered, "Like…like a complete lizard."

J. D. Turner, avowed bachelor, still enjoyed the fact that his charms could turn heads and make hearts beat faster. A lizard? He could hardly believe his ears. He was tempted to kiss her again, even if it did earn him another wallop with the purse.

He studied her more closely.

Well, no wonder she was showing immunity to his charms. Her close physical resemblance to Elana had made him assume she was like Elana.

But a closer inspection showed she wasn't.

That blouse was buttoned right up to her throat. Her hair had been forced into a tight no-nonsense bun. Her makeup was understated. Her lips were pursed into an expression of disapproval that was distinctly schoolmarm-ish.

"What can I do for you?" he asked, curtly. She might not be Elana, but she was of Elana. A relative. Maybe a twin sister. No, a younger sister. But whoever she was, nothing about Elana was going to be good news. He felt that right down to his gut.

She released an arm from where it guarded her wet breast, and swiped at her lips as if removing germs from them. Her arm returned immediately to its guard position. Then she looked around, and he saw it register in her eyes that she was on the front porch of a strange house with a near-naked man who had just kissed her, and the nearest neighbor was not within shouting distance.

Under different circumstances, he most certainly would have tried to reassure her. But Elana meant danger.

Even if this woman in front of him looked like the least dangerous person in the world, he had tasted her lips. There was something in that kiss that was not nearly as cool as she was purporting to be.

Her hair, the color of ripening wheat, piled up primly, still framed a face so beautiful she could be mistaken for an angel. Of course, Elana could have been mistaken for an angel, too.

He saw now his visitor was slender. Elana had been slender, too, but somehow voluptuous at the same time. And Elana had liked the sexy look, miniskirts, black leather. His present visitor's tailored suit reinforced that impression of a schoolmarm. The pastel blue reminded him of something his dental hygienist wore. The whole package screamed "prim and proper," Mary Poppins arriving at her assignment.

Elana had not been prim and proper. Still, the danger crackled in the air around this less vivacious copy.

"What can I do for you?" he repeated, his voice deliberately cold.

"Nothing," she decided. "I've made a mistake." She took a shaky step backwards, and then turned to flee.

He didn't honestly know whether he felt regret or relief that the mystery of his visitor was going to go unsolved.

He supposed he was leaning a bit toward regret, since he had to bite back the "wait" that wanted to pop out of his mouth.

In her haste to get away from him, she stumbled on the second stair. Instinct made him reach for her, but it was too late. She went flying; he could hear the dull thud of her head hitting the cement pad at the bottom of the steps.

He was at her side in an instant, animosity forgotten.

She looked at him, dazed. "Don't touch me," she ordered groggily.

Her forehead was cut, a lump growing around the cut at an alarming speed.

"Don't touch me," she ordered again, as he picked her up. She was so light, it didn't strain his hurt shoulder to lift her. Her weight was unexpectedly warm and sweet in his arms.

"Put me down," she demanded, then had to close her

eyes, the effort of making that small demand too much for her.

He ignored her, tried to ignore the fact the towel was slipping dangerously, and carried her back up the steps. He coaxed the screen door open with his toe, and went through to the kitchen. He set her in a chair, instantly feeling the cold where her warmth had puddled against his chest.

She tried to stand up. He noticed, even with all the excitement, she was managing to keep her wet chest protected from his gaze.

"Sit," he ordered, sternly and then did some quick adjustments to the towel.

She gave him a defiant look, took one wobbly step toward the door, and then sank reluctantly back down in the chair. Her eyes darted around his kitchen, which was not in the running for a *Better Homes and Gardens* feature.

The room was plainly furnished—Formica table, steel-framed chairs with burgundy vinyl padding. His dishes—three or four days worth—were piled in the sink. Her gaze came to rest, with faint disapproval, on the engine he had taken apart on his countertop.

J.D. thought that was just like a woman to be noticing the decorating—or lack thereof—at the very same time she was entertaining the idea she was in mortal danger.

His dog, Beauford, a nice mix between a coonhound and a basset, had been sleeping under the table. He chose that moment to rise on stubby legs, stretch his solid black, white and brown body, and then plop his huge head on her lap. He sniffed impolitely, blinked appealingly with his sad brown eyes, and began to drool.

She squealed, dropping her arms from their defense position across her chest, and pushed the dog's head out of her lap.

"Filthy beast," she said, staring at the new wet spot on her pants.

Okay. J.D. could tolerate a lot, and he knew Beauford had a tendency to have bad breath, and he drooled, but that did not a filthy beast make. This was about as much of the home invasion as he could tolerate.

He held up his fingers. He would pronounce her medically sound, and then it was out of here for Miss Priss. Filthy beast, indeed. "How many?"

"Three," she said, once again folding her arms over the wet spot on her blouse and glaring at him.

"What day is it?"

"June 28."

"What day were you born?"

"How would you know if I had that right?"

Good point. And the fact that she could make it probably meant her brain wasn't too badly addled. Time to send her on her way.

But she looked like just the type who would sue if she ended up with a concussion or something so he reluctantly turned from her and got a pack of frozen peas out of the freezer compartment of his fridge. He placed it on the bump on her head, and held it. She closed her eyes, briefly, and then struggled to get up again.

"Just relax," he said, holding her down with one finger on her shoulder. "I'm not going to hurt you."

"Then why did you do that?" she asked. Her bosom was heaving sweetly under the thin, wet blouse.

For a moment he thought she was accusing him of knocking her down the stairs. "What exactly did I do?" he snapped.

"You kissed me!"

"Oh, that." He shrugged, as if it meant nothing, when in actual fact the taste of her lips was lingering sweetly on his mouth. "I thought you were someone else."

She pondered that, and understanding dawned in the violet depths of her eyes. It was clear she now understood the passionate nature of his relationship with her look-alike.

"You are Jed Turner, aren't you?"

He tried not to flinch when she said that. Only Elana had ever called him Jed. Everyone else called him J.D.

"John," he corrected her. "Or J.D. J. D. Turner."

"I'm Tally Smith. I believe you knew my older sister, Elana," she said, finding her voice, sticking her chin out at him as if to prove she wasn't afraid, when she was trembling like a leaf on a silver aspen.

He waited, holding the bag on her forehead, not having any intention of making anything any easier for her.

"I knew her briefly." He kept his voice curt, devoid of emotion, not a hint in that cold tone of a man who had once sung a love song.

She took a deep breath, contemplated, and then plunged. "She died."

Two words. He registered them slowly. And realized that for him, Elana had died a long time ago.

He didn't know what to say. That he was sorry? He was not sure that he was. He was glad when the phone rang, giving him a chance to think. He took Tally Smith's hand—which was small, and soft and warm—and put it over the frozen bag of peas, then turned to the phone.

"Mrs. Saddlechild? Yeah. It's ready. Ten bucks. I'll bring it over tomorrow. My pleasure." He hung up the phone, wishing it had been a longer call, maybe Clyde phoning to consult about the Mustang, something, *anything,* that required more of him.

And then he turned back to her. Tally Smith, Elana's kid sister. Tally looked to be in her mid-twenties. Elana had been his own age, which was thirty now.

She was out of the chair, easing her way, shakily, toward the door. The peas were still pressed obediently against her forehead.

"When did she die?" he asked, reluctantly.

Her eyes were cloudy with pain, and he didn't think it had all that much to do with the bump on her head.

"Nearly a year ago."

"And why are you telling me? And why now?"

"I don't know," she said.

He could hear something in her voice. It had been in Elana's voice, too. Mysterious, faintly seductive. But in her voice he could hear smokey mountains, dark green hills, deep, clear water.

Or maybe that was a John Denver song. Elana had come from a prairie town, not very different from this one, across the Canadian border.

"Are you from Saskatchewan?" he asked her.

She nodded.

"You came a long way to tell me." He could explain to her that he hadn't seen her sister for years. And that he had known her only briefly. But it seemed to him this stranger in his kitchen was not entitled to know any of the details surrounding his heartbreak.

She looked at him, hard, and he knew, sinkingly, she did know why she had come. She just wasn't saying.

"Yes, I did come a long way" she said stiffly, and despite the stiffness, he saw the weariness in her. The dog padded after her as if she was his best friend. She gave Beauford a look of distaste, and the teaspoon of sympathy he'd been feeling for her evaporated. What kind of cold-hearted person could dislike Beauford with his beautiful, soulful eyes and slowly wagging stub of a tail?

J.D. followed her out the door, holding the dog back on the top of the steps. She negotiated them without incident this time. He glanced beyond her, and saw a little gray Nissan. It looked like an older model. Those cars went forever. He made note of the Canadian plate.

"You should have used the phone," he said, unsympathetically.

People did not come a long way to tell you bad news without a reason. He'd tangled his life briefly with a Smith girl five years ago. And he felt he'd been lucky to get out alive. He wasn't tangling with another one. It didn't matter if she was temperamentally Elana's polar opposite. Whatever she'd come here for, she wasn't getting it.

She hesitated at the gate, stopped and looked back at him. He could see the struggle on her face. She wanted to tell him something.

And he knew whatever it was, he didn't want to hear it.

"Nice of you to drop by," he said, pointedly. "Don't let the gate hit you in the backside on the way out."

She got the hint. But rather than seeming perturbed by his rudeness, did she look relieved? As if she wanted him to be rude and rough and rotten?

He frowned at her.

Her shoulders set proudly, she walked down the pathway to her car. She was no Elana, but even so, he was irritated that everything that was male in him noticed the easy grace of her walk, the casual unconscious sensuality in the way she moved. While her back was to him, he wiped the last tantalizing traces of her from his lips.

She got in the car and sat there for a moment looking

at him. He looked right back. She blinked first, started the car and backed up.

He stood on his porch in his towel, his arms folded across his chest, watching until her car was well out of sight. J.D. hoped that was the last he was ever going to see of a Smith girl, but he had an ugly feeling that he was being wishful.

He realized, that despite the swipe with his arm, he could still taste the cool sweetness of her lips on his mouth. He wiped ferociously before he went back in to finish his shower.

Annabel the cow had lost her appeal entirely. He showered in smoldering silence.

"You should be relieved," Tally Smith told herself on the short drive back to the town of Dancer. "He is not the right man for the job. Not even close."

Despite the firmness with which she made that statement, she felt woozy and she hoped the bump on the head was all that was to blame.

But she knew it wasn't.

It was the fury of that kiss. The pure, unbridled passion of it.

"Ugh," she told herself, but she felt like she was a bad actress reading a required line in a play. J. D. Turner's mouth on hers had been appallingly delicious. If she hadn't come to her senses in time to hit him with her purse, she was not sure what the outcome might have been.

She had the awful feeling that something wild in her might have risen up to meet his fury, and his passion.

"Ugh," she said, again, with even less conviction than the last time.

His arms around her had taken her captive, held her

tight to his hard masculine body like bands of steel. She
had been forced to feel his slippery wet skin, the rock
hardness of pure muscle under that skin. The effect, in
combination with the unrestrained sensuality of his lips,
had been rather dizzying. Really, any self-respecting
woman in this day and age should not have reacted with
fervor to such a primitive display of strength and aggres-
sion.

But she had a feeling that might have been fervor she
felt—that heat and trembling at her core—right before
smacking the man with her purse.

"He is not the man for the job," she repeated out loud,
as if she was trying to convince her weaker self. Her
weaker self that might have actually liked that kiss. A
little bit.

She tapped her fingers on the steering wheel, lifted one
up. "One," she said. "He came to the door dressed in a
towel."

Rather than seeing that as a fault, her weaker self in-
sisted on recalling that picture in all its lewd detail.

J. D. Turner had looked like some ancient and ferocious
warrior. With a faint shudder, that she tried unsuccessfully
to convince herself was revulsion, she recalled his thick
dark hair wet and curling, his dark eyes smoldering, the
firm unforgiving line of his mouth. His naked skin was
bronzed and unblemished, his shoulders massive, his chest
carved. He was flat-bellied and long-legged. In other
words, he was totally intimidating, fiercely masculine, and
gloriously strong.

Nothing about the worn photo she had found among
Elana's things, when she had finally found the energy to
begin sorting through stuff, had prepared her for the reality of the man.

Oh, in the picture J. D. Turner had been handsome, but

his vitality, his essence had not been captured. He'd been dressed in faded jeans, and a white shirt, open at the throat. He'd had his backside braced against the hood of a car, one leg bent at the knee resting on the bumper, his arms folded across his chest. That shock of dark brown hair had been falling carelessly over his forehead, and his eyes had engaged the camera unself-consciously, deep and dark, laughter-filled. His grin had seemed boyish and open, faintly devil-may-care.

When she had heard the song, robust and raspy, bursting out the windows of that tiny house, she had thought she had found the man in the photograph.

But there had been nothing boyish or open about the angry man who had appeared at the door in a towel, and that she had just left, near-naked, and perturbingly unself-conscious about it, on his porch. No laughter in the dark brown of his eyes, no suggestion of a grin around the firmness of those lips.

She shivered thinking of the water beading on the sleek perfect muscles of his chest, of the way his flat belly slid into that towel, of the strength in those naked legs. When he had crossed his arms across his chest, the biceps had bulged, and the muscles of his forearm had rippled with a masculine strength and ease that had made Tally go weak at the knees. No wonder she had stumbled off his porch.

And no wonder Elana had succumbed to him, not that Tally wanted to start thinking about that.

"Stop it," she ordered herself. "He will not do. Answering the door in a towel was bad enough. But his kitchen was a disaster, and his dog was poorly behaved and stinky. J. D. Turner was rude, disrespectful and nasty! He won't do. Won't. Won't. Won't."

Taking a deep steadying breath, doing her best to clear

the residue of J. D. Turner from her mind, Tally drove slowly and deliberately the one mile back into Dancer, North Dakota.

Even though the town was like an oasis of green in the prairie gold that surrounded it, Tally could not really imagine a town less likely to be called Dancer.

"Sleeper would be more like it," she muttered, passing the tiny boxlike houses slumbering under the only gigantic trees for miles. The only sign of life was an ancient dog who lifted his head, mildly interested, when she drove by. She was willing to bet he stank, too.

Finally, she pulled into the motel. For some reason it was called Palmtree Court, even though there was no court, and the nearest palm tree was probably several hundred miles south. Well, if a sleepy town could be called Dancer, why not stretch the truth a little further?

The Palmtree Court was a collection of humble little cabins, and it was the only commercial accommodation available in Dancer. Tally had woken up the clerk, an old man snoozing in a rocker behind the desk, earlier. Once awake, he had shown an inordinate interest in prying her life story from her, but she had closed her cabin door with most of her secrets still intact.

She had been relieved to see that despite the modest exterior, her cabin was clean and cozy. The quilt on the bed, on closer inspection proved to be handmade.

She went in now, and sank down on the bed. Ridiculously, she was still in possession of J.D.'s peas, and she put them over the bump on her head.

"I should call Herbert this moment," she said, but she did not pick up the phone.

Herbert Henley was, after all, the front-running candidate for the job. On her birthday, three months ago, he had put a tasteful diamond ring—nothing ostentatious—

on her finger. But that had been before Tally had had the god-awful luck to find that photo of a laughing J. D. Turner.

Herbert owned Henley's Hardware store. He never dressed in towels. He owned a neat-as-a-pin home in the historic district of Dogwood Hollow, Saskatchewan. Even in the comfort of his home he always wore a nice shirt and that adorable bow tie that had made her notice him in the first place. And he would never in a million years have taken an engine to pieces on his kitchen counter. He took great pride in his kitchen, especially his stainless steel appliances. He shared her dislike for dogs, and owned a prize-winning Persian cat named Bitsy-Mitsy.

That was quite a different picture than J.D.'s Engine Repair, where the little white house was nearly lost among overgrown lilacs. The house needed a coat of paint and was overshadowed by a large gray tin shop. The grass was too long around the several open sheds that contained monster machinery that she thought might have been combines.

Though she didn't necessarily believe that neatness pertained to character, the fact that he'd also answered the door in a towel and then kissed a perfect stranger were adding up to a pretty complete picture.

Then there was the fact that J.D. had not been wearing a wedding ring.

"That doesn't pertain to character, either," she told herself, adjusting the peas, which were starting to defrost. Did her noticing the lack of a wedding ring mean she was still considering him as a possibility?

How could she be so foolish? She had always considered herself the person least likely to be foolish.

And foolishness was what she could least afford now

that she was embarked on this task of such monumental importance.

"This is the most important thing I've ever done," she reminded herself sternly. In all fairness to J. D. Turner, perhaps she could not cross him off her list because she had caught him at a bad moment.

Okay, he'd accosted a complete stranger with his lips, but he had mistaken her for her sister. And he had come to the door wearing only a towel, but he'd probably thought she was one of his buddies. Dancer didn't look like the type of place where too many strangers showed up on doorsteps.

He'd had an engine on the counter, but maybe that wasn't a fatal flaw. And the dog was horrible, but at least it was friendly, which was more than she could say about Bitsy-Mitsy.

She'd come all this way. She could not let emotion cloud her reason now. The man was her nephew's biological father, and her all-important task, her life mission, had become to find Jed a father.

She had known who J. D. Turner was from the instant she had found his picture among her sister's things. He was the father of Elana's son, Jed.

And now, since Elana's death, Tally was Jed's legal guardian. Her life now was about doing what was right by that child. Her child. She had begun researching how to raise a happy and well-adjusted child as soon as he came to her. She'd been dismayed to learn happy, well-adjusted children came largely from happy, well-adjusted families, with *two* parents. She had been further dismayed to learn that the same-sex parent had a particularly important role in a child's development.

Since then, she'd been conducting an informal father search all over Dogwood Hollow and beyond. Her plan

was simple—she would systematically find the right father for her nephew, marry him and create a perfect family. She saw it as a good thing that emotion was not cloud-
ing the issue. She'd seen what too much emotion could
do in a life, namely Elana's.

Herbert Henley, solid, practical, infinitely stable was
her choice.

Until she had found that photograph. And then her
sense of fair play had said that the man in the picture at
least deserved a shot at being a father to the son he obviously had no idea he had sired.

So, she'd come here to Dancer to meet him. Well, he'd
made a bad first impression, but what if that wasn't the
whole story? Someday, when her nephew Jed was older,
she would be accountable for the decisions she was making right now.

Her decisions had to be cool and pragmatic, based on
fact, not impulse. So, despite her initial reaction, tomorrow she would interview J. D. Turner's friends and neighbors. She prayed she would find out J.D. was a beer-
swilling swine with three ex-wives and a criminal record.
And then she could go home and happily marry Herbert,
her conscience clear.

Though, she wished, suddenly, wearily, she could put
the lid back on that box she had opened, and never find
that photo with the name Jed Turner written in her sister's
hand on the back of it.

Chapter Two

J.D., lying flat on his back underneath a car, gave a mighty heave, ignoring the pain in his shoulder, and the rusted bolt finally came loose. He took it off with much more vengeance than was strictly required, and tossed it aside. Then the phone rang and he bumped his head on the oil pan.

Not a good day, so far, he thought, sliding out from under the car. He glanced at the clock. And he was a full five minutes into it.

"J.D.'s," he answered abruptly, cradling the phone in his ear while he wiped the grease off his hands.

"Stan here."

Where were you last night when I needed it to be you standing at the door instead of her?

"What do you want?"

"Geez. Nice greeting."

"I'm having a bad day."

"It's five after eight!"

"I know."

"Well, this should cheer you up. There was this stranger in the Chalet this morning having breakfast. Female. Kind of cute in the librarian sort of way. You know the kind where a guy thinks about pulling the pins from her hair—"

"And this news would cheer me up for what reason?" J.D. cut off his friend before he went too far down the pulling-pins-from-her-hair road. He knew full well that was a path of thought that could make a man spend the whole night wide awake and staring at his ceiling.

Pins from her hair, lace under a sheer damp blouse, eyes an unreal color of indigo, these were all thoughts that ultimately led to heads banged on oil pans first thing in the morning.

"Because," Stan said with glee, obviously saving the best for last, "Guess who the librarian slash goddess was asking about?"

"Fred Basil?" J.D. asked hopefully. Fred was another town bachelor. He was sixty-two, built like a beach ball and changed his overalls once a year whether he needed to or not. He had politely declined joining the A.G.M.N.W.N.C., saying he would like to get married if the right gal came along.

"Guess again, good buddy," Stan said, his good cheer bordering on the obnoxious.

J.D.'s head started to hurt. He hoped it was a delayed reaction to hitting it on the oil pan, but he knew it wasn't. He prided himself on leading a nice quiet life. Simple. Devoid of intrigues and mysteries. A man such as himself did not probe this kind of gossip. He rose above it. Performing at his best, J.D. would have said a firm goodbye and hung up the phone. Maybe he could blame the oil pan for the regrettable fact that he was not performing at his best, and he did not hang up the phone. But he suspected it was more pins and lace and indigo eyes.

"I'll give you a hint," Stan said sagely to J.D.'s silence. "You might have to think of relinquishing your membership in the A.G.M.N.W.N. Club."

J.D. said three words in a row that would have made a sailor blush. Those three words were followed by a terse sentence. "What the hell kind of questions is she asking?" Five minutes later he hung up the phone, fury burning like coal chunks in his stomach. She had crossed the line. It wasn't enough that she had caught him at a bad moment yesterday, singing his fool head off, wrapped in a towel.

Oh, no, now she had to publicly connect herself with him, provide all sorts of gossip to the eager mongers of the village. She was embarrassing him. She was invading his privacy. Enough was enough. He had no choice.

The sane thing, of course, would be to ignore her, to rise above.

The insane thing would be to track her down and tell her, like a sheriff in a bad Western, that this was his town and there wasn't room for the both of them. Of course, he did the insane thing, stoking his fury all the way to town.

Of all the nerve! Asking sneaky questions about him to his friends and neighbors.

The Nissan was not parked at the Palmtree and was no longer in front of the Chalet. J.D. felt a moment's hope that Tally Smith had gone away, but he knew he wouldn't sleep well until he knew that for sure. Even after he'd confirmed her departure it occurred to him the pins-out-of-her-hair thoughts might plague him for awhile.

He began a slow patrol of Dancer's eight blocks of residential streets.

Sure enough, there was her little gray Nissan parked in front of Mrs. Saddlechild's house. He was willing to bet it was no coincidence it was parked there because he had made the mistake of uttering Mrs. Saddlechild's name when he spoke to her on the phone last night, while that spy had been ensconced in his camp, with his frozen peas on her head.

He went up to her door and knocked hard on it.

Mrs. Saddlechild looked as ancient as the lawn mower he had repaired for her. Today, she was dressed in a flowered housedress, her hair newly blue, her smudged glasses sliding off the end of her nose.

"Just in the garden shed, J.D., thanks," she said briskly, through a crack in the door. And then she closed her door in his face.

She thought he was delivering her lawn mower!

He frowned. He could go and wait in his truck for Ms. Tally Smith to come out. He could pull all the wires out from under the dash of her car so that she couldn't escape without answering a few questions, without hearing that he was running her out of town.

He could do all that, but it would be too close to playing her silly little game of cloak-and-dagger.

Plus, there was no telling what Mrs. Saddlechild was telling the insatiably curious Tally Smith. Mrs. Saddlechild had seen him naked, for God's sake, and it was possible she was old enough and addled enough to forget the all-important detail that he'd been three years old at the time.

The front door had three little panes of frosted glass in it. He glanced up and down the block, and then peered in one of them.

The house seemed very dark in comparison to the bright sunshine outside. Still, after a moment, he could see through to the kitchen, where windows were letting light in.

There was a huge platter of cookies on the kitchen table. Mrs. Saddlechild always had cookies for him when he delivered the mower. As he watched, a slender hand reached out and took one. He was sure he caught the briefest glimpse of bright blond hair before it moved back out of range of his vision.

Just as he'd suspected, Tally Smith was in there! Eating *his* cookies. Talking to a woman who'd known him since he was a baby, a woman who had personal information about him that could be both embarrassing and damaging.

What the hell did Tally Smith want? He banged on the door again.

Mrs. Saddlechild came, opened her door that same cautious crack, and peered at him, annoyed. "You're still here, J.D.?"

"Apparently," he said.

"Oh, your money!"

Yeah, like he'd been standing out here on her porch waiting for ten dollars

"This is not about your lawn mower," he said with poorly disguised impatience. "I want to speak to your guest."

Mrs. Saddlechild eyed him warily, and closed the door without inviting him in. It seemed like an awfully long time before she returned.

"It's not convenient right now," she said.

"It damn well better become convenient," J.D. said. "You tell her—"

"J. D. Turner! When she told me you had not behaved like a gentleman toward her, I barely believed it. But here you are on my step, cursing." She shook her head and made a little sucking sound with her lips.

He could see his future unfolding dismally before his eyes. All the senior citizens in Dancer would be looking at him sideways now. He'd have to do free lawn mower tune-ups for a year to remove this smudge from his character.

That woman in there was ruining his life without half-trying.

"Kindly tell her I'll be waiting," he said tautly.

Mrs. Saddlechild sniffed regally and snapped her door shut. He figured he'd be cooling his heels for a good hour, and so he was relieved when Tally appeared a few moments later.

"Yes?" she said, stepping out onto the porch.

His relief was short-lived. Her hair was in the same crisp bun of the pulling-the-pins-from-it fantasy. She was wearing a crisp white shirt that was not silk, and pressed navy blue shorts that ended at the dimple in her knee. It reminded him of the kind of outfit lady golfers or off-duty nuns wore.

If you did not know there was a lacy bra underneath it, it was the kind of outfit designed to inspire trust and nothing else.

"Don't 'yes?' me in that innocent tone of voice," he warned her. He looked at her eyes, thinking last night's fading light must have lent illusion to the color. But no, they were more purple than blue. Amazing.

The cool light in them made him want to pull all the pins from her hair.

"Leona said she'd call the police if you didn't mind your manners."

Leona. Great. This was just great. Was that actually a twinkle of amusement warming her eyes? How dare she be amused at his expense?

"I want to know what the hell you think you are doing," he said, his tone low. He could see Mrs. Saddlechild peering out from behind her front curtain. He smiled for her benefit, but the smile felt stretched and taut, like a wolf baring its teeth.

"I'm having tea," Tally said, unforthcoming. "And ginger snaps."

He wanted to grab her and shake her until the pins flew free. Or kiss her again. He tried to remember the last time he had felt this passionate—this uncomfortably out-of-control—but the answer evaded him. "Why are you doing this? Why are you asking questions about me? Why are you so hell-bent on creating problems in my life?"

Her eyes were very expressive, and she looked guilty, a kid caught with her hand in the cookie jar, but she said, her tone dignified, "I don't see how asking a few innocent questions could create problems in your life."

"Really? Well let me tell you something. When a stranger shows up in Dancer and starts asking if J. D. Turner pays his bills on time, by the next day it's the talk of the coffee shop that he probably gambled away his life savings in Las Vegas."

The guilty look darkened her eyes, so he pressed onward, "And if somebody asks if he has an ex-wife or two stashed away somewhere, then the talk in the barbershop and the hairdresser's for the next three weeks will be about the possibility that he might have a secret wife or two. People will begin to 'remember' little incidents that back up this theory. There will be sightings in nearby towns."

"Surely you exaggerate," she said uncertainly, and looked guiltier than ever.

"And does J. D. Turner get drunk on Friday night? Or Monday? Or Tuesday? I guarantee you, there will be lookouts outside the New Life Church where AA meets twice a week for the next year trying to catch me making an entrance.'' He was enjoying her guilt, immensely, the fact that she had dropped her gaze from him and was now studying the toe of a sneaker so absurdly white she must have polished it.

"And let's not forget the final question. Does J. D. Turner like children? Good God, that coupled with me tracking you down here will have Mrs. Saddlechild posting the wedding bans in the *Dancer Daily News!*"

He saw, suddenly, and with grave irritation, she had not lowered her eyes from his out of guilt alone. Her shoulders were shaking suspiciously.

"Are you laughing?"

She glanced up at him, and shook her head, vehemently, no. But it was too late. He had seen the line of her mouth curve up, the mischievous sparkle it brought to her eyes.

"I fail to see the humor in this," he said sternly. Thankfully, she quit smiling. That smile would make it way too easy to forget she was an uptight menace, and that his mission was to run her out of town.

She looked at him squarely, drew back her shoulders. "You don't strike me as a man who gives two hoots about what the people of this town have to say about you."

"Just because you've been digging up dirt, don't assume you know one single thing about me, Tally Smith."

"As a matter of fact," she said, and he did not miss her reluctance, "there is no dirt. You appear to be a highly respected member of this community."

"Your tone implies I have somehow managed to pull the wool over the eyes of an entire town."

"Apparently most of whom have been spared the sight of you in a towel. And also," she continued, "as a charter member of the Ain't Gettin' Married, No Way, Never

Club, it strikes me as bizarre that you would kiss a complete stranger on your front porch."

Stan had a big mouth. The club was secret!

"Kissing has nothing to do with marriage, unless you read a certain kind of novel, which I am almost certain you do." He had scored, because he saw indignant red splotches bloom in her cheeks. "Plus, for as fascinating as all this is, you haven't answered my original question. Why the curiosity in the first place?"

She looked at the toe of her shoe again. So did he. The whiteness of those runners really bugged him. Didn't she have anything better to do with her time?

Didn't she have a fellow chasing her around trying to get the pins out of her hair?

He reminded himself firmly, that only one question about her was any of his business. The question that pertained to him. Everything else entered distinctly murky territory.

"Cat got your tongue?" he asked silkily. "I want an answer. I want to know why you've been asking questions about me all over town."

"All right," she said. "My sister left you a small inheritance. I wanted to see if you deserved it. I'll mail it to you."

He watched with extreme interest as the tip of her nose turned red, and then her earlobes, and then her neck.

He was willing to bet she had never told a lie before in her life.

"Try again," he said, folding his arms over his chest, and giving her the mean look that always made Stan flub his pool shot.

She took a deep breath and looked everywhere but at him. She touched the button at her throat to make sure it was done up tight, not an ounce of her exposed to him.

"I found your picture in my sister's things," she said finally, her tone clipped and uneasy.

"And?"

"And I was intrigued. I wanted to know more." Her glowing red nose and earlobes changed to a shade of beet.

"Don't even try to appeal to my male ego," he said. "It won't work. There is no way you drove all this way because you looked at a picture and found me irresistibly attractive. You could have any guy you blinked your big eyes at back home, wherever that is. You wouldn't have to drive halfway across the country looking for one."

"I wasn't trying to appeal to your male ego," she said indignantly. "I have a man at home. I most likely will marry him before the year is out."

Her enthusiasm for her upcoming nuptials was underwhelming. She sounded like a Victorian maiden, in one of those books he was positive she read, who'd been promised against her will. So much for a guy chasing after her trying to get her to let her hair down.

Not that J. D. Turner wanted the details of her excruciatingly boring love life. Not that he wanted to even think why the flatness of her statement made him feel an unwanted stab of sympathy coupled with a desire to kiss her all over again.

"I want the truth. A hard concept for you and your sister, I know, but I'm not settling for anything less."

"Please don't say anything bad about my sister."

The sudden ache in her voice, the tenderness nearly undid him more than her emotionless announcement of her upcoming marriage.

"Elana was sick," she said quietly.

Ah, the truth, finally. "Well, you said she died. I assumed she was sick first."

"No. She died in a car accident. She was sick all her life. She had a mental disorder."

"Elana?" he said incredulously.

"Sometimes she hurt the people who loved her. She didn't mean to."

"Elana?" he said, again.

Tally nodded. "You probably met her in an upswing. Lots of energy? Incredible enthusiasm? Unbelievable zest for life?"

He was staring at her, openmouthed.

"Everybody loved her when she was like that," Tally said, almost gently.

"I never said I loved her," he said fiercely.

"I think you did, though." No glow to her ears and nose, no color blooming at the base of her slender throat now, when he most needed it!

"That's ridiculous. Why would you think that?"

"Because of the picture I found." She faltered. "And because of the way you kissed me when you thought it was her."

If he'd been a really smart man, he would have hung his Gone Fishin' sign on the shop door after Stan's phone call this morning and taken off for a week or two. All this would have blown over by the time he got back.

But he had not done that, and now he bulldozed on, determined to get to the truth, more determined than ever to see Tally Smith riding off into the sunset.

"You still seem to be dodging around the question. Let me put this very simply. What is Tally Smith doing in Dancer, North Dakota?"

"I wanted to find out some things about the man my sister loved."

He snorted. "She didn't love me."

"I think she did. That's probably why she left you. She

started to go down. Loved you enough that she didn't want you to see it.''

He looked at her closely. Little tears were shining behind her eyes. He wasn't the only one Elana Smith had caused pain to. Tally had said everyone loved her sister when she was up. He suspected very few people had loved her when she was down.

The last thing he wanted to do was see Tally in a sympathetic light because it blurred his resolve. On the other hand, her man wasn't chasing her trying to get her hair down, and she had coped with a sick sister.

"I'm sorry she was sick," he heard himself saying. "I really am, Tally."

She blinked rapidly, and then said, way too brightly, "Anyway, I've found out all I wanted to know. You'll be happy to know I'm leaving first thing tomorrow morning. No more questions."

"I am happy to know that," he said, but he didn't feel completely happy or completely convinced, either.

"Goodbye, J.D.," she said. She stuck out her hand.

He made the mistake of taking it. He felt a little shiver of desire for her, the smallest regret it was over before it ever started.

He yanked his hand away and went back down Mrs. Saddlechild's walk more troubled than when he had gone up it. Something was wrong here.

But he'd gotten what he wanted, an assurance she was leaving. He went home and went back to work. He ate supper and showered, no singing. Unease niggled at the back of his mind, as if he had missed a piece of the puzzle, as if he should know something that he didn't. He felt as if she had never given him the real answer to why she was here, but that if he just thought hard enough, he would figure it out.

When no answer came, he ordered himself over and over to forget it. But as soon as he let down his guard, the unanswered question filled his mind again.

He went to sleep nursing it.

J.D. woke deep in the night, moonlight painting a wide stripe across his bedroom floor, the cry of a coyote still echoing in the air, lonesome and haunting. He lay still, aware of the deep rise and fall of his own chest, feeling momentarily content.

But then the question he had gone to sleep pondering swept back into his mind, and the contentment was gone, like dust before a broom.

Why was Tally Smith *really* here? Beyond driving him crazy? And beyond getting the citizenry of Dancer worked up into a nice gossiping frenzy, the likes of which had not been seen since Mary Elizabeth Goodwin, prom queen, had gotten pregnant without the benefit of marriage almost a half-dozen summers ago.

All this nonsense about Tally wanting to see who her sister had loved, about being intrigued by a photograph, just did not add up. Elana might have been compulsive, but her little sister looked cautious, organized, *responsible*.

The person least likely to act on an impulse.

For some reason Tally Smith was lying, or at the very best, not telling him the full truth. He could see it in her eyes—and in her ears and nose and throat, come to that. In the darkness of his room, he allowed himself the luxury he had not allowed himself during the day. J.D. contemplated the color of her eyes.

They were astounding, shifting from indigo to violet, sending out beacons when she felt guilty and troubled. He thought of that one moment when she had smiled, and a brief light had chased the somberness from her eyes.

The coyote howled again, and the sound shivered in the night, and that shiver went up and down J.D.'s spine, and stopped at the base of his neck. It tickled there, a premonition that his life was about to change in ways he could have never imagined.

Why was she asking people if he liked children?

Had there been the tiniest bit of truth threaded through her statement that Elana had left him an inheritance?

And then he knew. With that clarity that comes in the night sometimes, in those moments partway between sleep and waking, he knew.

He sat up, his heart racing crazily.

He tried to tell himself it couldn't be, that it was not even possible, but he failed utterly to convince himself. A sense of urgency overcame him, and he tossed back the tangle of sheets and blankets and put his feet on the floor. He hoped the cold would slam him back into reality, but the sense of urgency did not abate.

Cursing, he pulled his jeans from a heap on the floor and yanked them on. He shoved his arms in the sleeves of his shirt as he ran for the truck, not stopping for shoes, barely aware of the rocks digging into his bare feet.

What if she hadn't waited until morning? What if she was gone already? He didn't know one single thing about her, except that she was Elana's sister and that she was from north of the border. How many Smiths would there be?

It wouldn't matter. If he'd missed her, if she had folded up her tent and slunk away in the night, he would track down every last Smith in Canada, until he had confirmed the truth that had unfolded in his heart and his head a few minutes ago.

He didn't bother to button the shirt, just started the truck and barreled toward town. Not much law enforce-

ment out this way at the best of times. None at—he
glanced at his watch—three-thirty in the morning. He
pressed down the accelerator, and watched with satisfaction when the needle jumped over ninety.

J. D. Turner knew how to rebuild a truck engine. If he
was as good at other things, it might not have taken him
so long to figure out why she was here.

The roar of the engine split the quiet of the prairie
night. He squealed his tires at the one stop sign on Main
Street. If he wasn't more careful, if all of Dancer wasn't
speculating about him and Tally Smith by now, they certainly would be soon.

He felt almost weak with relief when he raced into the
parking lot of the Palmtree and saw the little gray Nissan
parked in front of a darkened cabin. It was the only car
at the Palmtree. Good. He didn't have to wake up everybody in the whole place banging on doors until he found
her.

He got out of his truck and hammered on the door
closest to her car, waited, hammered again.

After a long moment, he saw movement at the cabin
window. The curtain flicked open ever so slightly and then
flicked back into place, swiftly. Silence. Not a hint of
movement outside, or inside either. He could picture her
standing with her back against the wall, palms flat against
it, holding her breath.

"Tally Smith, I know you're awake." It was a challenge to find the right voice volume—one she would hear,
but not the rest of the town.

Silence.

"Open this door right now or I'm breaking it down."
This a little louder.

More silence. After all her research, she should really
know better than to try calling his bluff.

"I'm counting to three." He was just a little short of the decibel level that made walls shake and blew out windows.

Did he hear a little scuffling noise on the other side of the door?

"One." He lowered his voice, marginally.

He heard the bolt move.

"Two."

The handle twisted.

"Thr—"

The door opened a crack, and she put one eye to it, and regarded him with grave annoyance.

"What are you doing?" she whispered. "You'll wake up everyone in town."

Her hair was spilling down around her shoulders in an untamed wave that gave complete lie to the long-sleeved, high-collared nightgown, straight off *Little House on the Prairie.*

"Let me in," he demanded.

"No. It's the middle of the night. Are you drunk?"

Drunk? "No, I am not drunk," he told her dangerously. "Isn't that somewhere in your notes? That J. D. Turner doesn't get drunk?"

She sniffed. "There's a first time for everything."

"You know, come to think of it, if I was going to get drunk, you would be a pretty good excuse."

"I'm not going to stand here in the middle of the night and be insulted by you." She tried to shut the door, but he slipped his foot in.

"We need to talk," he told her.

"It will have to wait until morning."

She was so bossy. This took on new and significant meaning now that he knew his life was going to be tangled with hers, one way or another, forever. "It's morning actually."

She opened the door all the way, and glared at his foot until he put it back on the other side where it belonged. Her hair was all sleep-messed. It looked exactly the way he had known it would had he been given a chance to remove the pins from it—thick and rich and wild, tumbling over her shoulders and softening the lines of her face. She looked more approachable. Sexy, actually.

He knew he must be mad, because he had that urge to kiss her again. Mad, angry. Mad, crazy, too.

"So," she said, tapping her foot, "talk."

She had a watch on and she glanced at it pointedly, to let him know her middle-of-the-night time was doled out thriftily. The cascading hair had not changed her tone of voice, nor her snippy attitude.

He said, with deliberate slowness, enunciating each word, "You didn't come here checking out your sister's lost loves." It was a statement, not a question, and she knew it.

Whatever sleepiness was left her in face was replaced by wariness. "And your theory is?" she asked tartly.

"She had a baby." That wasn't a question, either. "My baby."

He saw the answer written in her face. The color drained from it so rapidly he thought she might faint. She stood frozen, her eyes huge and frightened.

In delayed reaction to his earlier decibel level, the light blinked on in the motel office. Some instinct for self-preservation made him take her shoulders. He guided her backward, inside the cabin. Then he closed the door and leaned on it.

"Boy or girl?" he asked, ice-cold.

"Boy," she whispered.

"I want to see my son. Get dressed. Because we are leaving right now."

Chapter Three

"We are not going anywhere," Tally said, finding her voice, and trying desperately to insert a note of steel into it. If this man ever got the upper hand, there would be no going back.

Though it must have been a mark of the lateness of the night, and the shock of his springing his newfound knowledge on her, that she could not think of what was so attractive about her life that she would need to go back to it.

J.D. glared at her, his eyes dark and challenging in the dim light of her room. She could see the strength and resolve in those eyes, and it occurred to her that there would be no winning a battle of wills with this man.

When she lost the staring contest, she dropped her eyes. Unfortunately, his shirt was unbuttoned and hanging open, revealing the broad and magnificent landscape of his chest. It occurred to her that she had seen more of J.D.'s chest than Herbert's, which was unseemly, given that she was planning an intimate lifelong relationship with Herbert. She shivered.

J.D. was a magnificent specimen of a man, and the anger that sizzled in the air around him did nothing to reduce his attraction. She could feel the power of him, vital and exciting, but that was exactly the type of thing that turned a woman's head, clouded her thinking. Being drawn to the unknown mysteries of a man was precisely the type of impulse that had gotten Elana into trouble again and again and again.

"Get dressed," he snapped, obviously mistaking her befuddlement for weakness. "And get packed."

She folded her arms over her chest. She could feel how rapidly her heart was beating, as if her very survival was being threatened by him taking control of her. But she wasn't going to let him know that she was thrilled and frightened in turn by this extraordinary twist in her plan.

"No," she said, giving herself a mental pat on the back for her calm tone. "You will have to haul me out of here, kicking and screaming." He seemed unmoved by that threat, and so she tacked on, "And won't that make a fine front page for the *Dancer Daily News*."

He leaned very close to her. She could feel his breath on her cheek, and it was warm and sensuous and dangerous. His eyes had a steely glint in them that did not bode well for her.

"I'll take that as a challenge, if you like," he said, his voice deceptively soft. "It wouldn't bother me one little bit to toss you over my shoulder and carry you out of here. You don't look like you'd weigh more than a sack of spuds. And I'm not worried about the *Dancer Daily*."

"That is not what you said earlier," she reminded him pertly.

"I was a different man then. My whole world has changed since then."

It felt like her whole world was shifting dangerously, too. She had to hold on to reason! She was always the one who made the plans, who knew what to do, who took charge. Surrendering was not an option.

Still, she tried a less aggressive stance. She softened her tone, touched his arm. "Could we be reasonable adults, here? There is no reason this can't wait until morning."

He was not the least taken in by the softer tone, and he glared at her fingers on his arm until she jerked her hand away. "Maybe you don't know this, but your sister led me to believe she was falling in love with me. And then she disappeared in the middle of the night, without even saying goodbye. So, I've been on the receiving end of a Smith girl's disappearing act before, and it's not happening again."

"You may have had a reason not to trust Elana, but I am not guilty by association. I have not given you a single reason not to trust me!"

All these years of respectability—Tally was a school teacher, for goodness sake—and still the fear lived in her, that people would look at her and see her sister, someone unworthy of their trust.

"I have a son that you didn't tell me about. That feels like a pretty good reason not to trust you. When were you going to tell me?"

When she was silent, he guessed, "Or maybe you had decided not to. Maybe I didn't pass the little daddy interviews you conducted around town. Maybe you decided, Miss Control, that you weren't going to tell me about the boy at all."

"I was so going to tell you," she said, but the truth

was when she had gone to bed this evening she had felt
entirely uncertain about what to do about the very trou-
bling Mr. J. D. Turner. It seemed telling him about Jed
had become all mixed up with the color of his eyes, and
the taste of his lips, and more than anything she wanted
to do what was right and rational.

"I bet you don't lie very often. That's probably why
the tip of your nose gets red when you fib. And then your
ears start to glow. And then your neck turns all red, right
here."

He touched her, his broad hand spanning her neck
where it joined her jawbone. She felt like a deer frozen
in headlights. She felt a compulsion to cover her nose and
ears, but she didn't have enough hands and it would have
been undignified, not to mention an admission of guilt.

"I was waiting for the right time," she stammered.

"The right time would have been on my front step."

"After you acted like a barbarian?" she sputtered. His
hand was still on her neck. It felt oddly gentle, given the
look in his eyes said he wanted to strangle her.

He seemed to realize he was still touching her, and he
pulled his hand away and glared at it as though it had
offended him.

"See?" he said wearily. "It's just as I suspected. You
were going to decide if I was suitable father material or
not, weren't you?" His hand must have wanted to strangle
her again, because he shoved it in his pocket.

"I was just trying to do what was best for my nephew,"
she defended herself, and she touched her neck where his
hand had been to see if it was truly burning.

"Well guess what? You've been retired as God. I'm
taking over. I'm in control now."

He pulled the hand out of his jean pocket, folded his
arms across his massive, naked chest and stared her down.

She waited for the black wave that would tell her death had come.

Instead, she noticed what he smelled like: faintly spicy and entirely manly. Heavenly. Maybe she had died after all.

It occurred to her, that since she was fighting for her very survival, rather than enjoying his admittedly fine scent, she should pick something up and throw it at him. Scream. Bring half the town running.

But a disgusting little thing had happened inside of her when he had said he was in control now. Instead of feeling like she was going to die, she actually felt faintly relieved!

It was the scariest thing she had ever felt, a weakness. She had never tolerated weakness in herself. How could she? She had always needed to be the strong one. She could never let him see this startling vulnerability she had unearthed in herself. She could hardly believe she had admitted it to herself. How could she be relieved that this big, angry stranger was ripping the reins of control from her?

She had to fight!

"It would be kidnapping if you forced me to go with you." It was her schoolteacher voice at its mightiest.

He smiled, a cruel smile, that made him menacing and so god-awful handsome it should have been illegal. He reminded her, suddenly, of a pirate. Oh Lord, with a patch over his eye and a saber in his hand he would be the most frightening man on the planet. Not to mention the sexiest. What kind of opponent was a schoolteacher for a pirate?

She drew herself up short. He was not a pirate! He was a mechanic! Losing her grip on reality would be of no help to anyone.

"I can't drive in the middle of the night," she said with sharp haughtiness. "I have night blindness."

He snorted derisively. "You think I was going to let you drive? I'm driving."

"You won't like driving that far with an unhappy woman," she said, and then realized sometime, somehow, entirely against her will, she had relinquished her position that she was not going at all.

"You know what? I'd walk over fire to see my son. So you, and your unhappiness, are a relatively small challenge to me."

She should have felt insulted. Instead she felt the strangest sensation in her chest at the fierce loyalty this man felt for the son he didn't know.

She had come to Dancer to see if he would be a suitable daddy for Jed. Better than Herbert. It had been a stupid plan. Impulsive and plainly not thought through properly. She had never considered the possibility that he was going to gain the upper hand, wrest control of the whole situation from her.

On the other hand, wasn't there a faint possibility that from the moment she had seen his picture she had known J. D. Turner was the man most likely to rescue her from the incredibly boring life she had planned for herself?

It was a renegade thought, and one she had to subdue immediately. She had seen, firsthand, thanks to Elana, what excitement did to people's lives!

"What my nephew needs most in his life is stability," she warned him. When J.D. looked unimpressed with her pronouncement, she added, "I read it in a book."

"Look, I can see you are one of those people who goes through life with an instruction manual, a complete set of world maps, a first aid kit, and a parachute, but sometimes it's okay just to create a plan as you go along. Be spontaneous."

Spontaneity didn't sound safe at all. If he'd lived his whole life with Elana he wouldn't be saying that.

"You need to know I am actively seeking a father for Jed," she said. Then she closed her eyes, commanded her courage and plunged. "I am committed to creating a normal, happy, healthy family for him." In case she hadn't been plain enough, she added. "That means a mother. And a father. Together."

The very thought of this particular mother and this particular father together in that particular way made the rest of her body catch up with her ears and nose and throat. Heat burned through her, from her toes to the very top of her head.

Not that he appeared to notice.

"Jed," he repeated, savoring the name. And then the rest of her statement caught up with him. His mouth dropped and snapped shut. He looked longingly at the door, but then he just took a deep breath, and met her gaze steadily. "And you need to know, I'm his father, but that doesn't change my position about getting married. Ever."

"Being a father is more than a function of biology and I wasn't proposing to you! Ugh! As it happens, I have a man picked out."

The "ugh" made him narrow his eyes and move even closer into her space. Their chests were nearly touching. She could feel heat rising from his body. Or maybe from her own.

"Is that who gave you the ring?"

He'd noticed the ring. What did that mean, exactly? "Yes," she said. "Herbert gave me the ring."

"Herbert," he repeated slowly, as if a name could tell him something. "So what are your criteria for a father for my son?" he asked.

"I want a man who is infinitely stable. Who is kind and considerate. Neat and tidy would help."

J.D.'s lip curled in derision.

"Well," she continued, "he won't run around in a towel for one thing. Or kiss complete strangers. He certainly won't have an engine dismantled in my kitchen!"

He leaned even closer. He planted one arm on either side of her head. His eyes were snapping with anger, but when his lips touched hers she did not feel anger. Or "ugh," which was probably the point of this exercise.

His lips were warm and sensuous. They tasted sweet and clean, like cold creek water. He nuzzled her mouth, until her lips parted ever so slightly and a strange, soft sigh came from her.

J. D. Turner was just much too sure of his charms. And not without reason. Her heart was pounding so hard inside her chest she thought she might collapse, slide her back right down the wall and sit herself down on the floor.

With great effort she stiffened her spine as he took his lips away.

"There," he said. "I've disqualified myself from your family plan, which by the way, I think is idiotic. That poor kid. He'll probably be raised in a home about as cozy as a military school based on your criteria for neat and tidy. A life of relentless nonadventure." It was his turn to say "ugh."

"I am giving Jed a wonderful life!" she said.

"You and Herbert, I assume. Do you polish his sneakers, too?"

"Herbert's or Jed's?"

"Boy, are you missing the point."

"I don't think the fact that I have clean sneakers should be seen as a mark against my character!"

"But the fact that I have an engine on my kitchen

counter should be a mark against mine?'' He looked at her lips again. Just his eyes on them was enough to make her shiver. ''The right man could make you forget all about the condition of your kitchen counters.''

''And that would not be you! You are the most aggravating person I have ever met!''

''Better get used to me, because it seems our lives are going to be tangled for a good long time to come.''

It occurred to her that was true. J.D. was part of her life now. He would be, from the look of determination on his face, a part of her life for as long as Jed was a part of her life.

And that was going to be forever.

She hadn't even made a conscious decision to include this horrible man in her life. It had just happened. Or had a conscious decision been made, way back in the safety of Dogwood Hollow, when she had looked at that photo of a laughing man leaning on a car?

''Let's go,'' he said, glancing at his watch, dismissing that kiss as easily as he would wave away a fly.

It truly made her want to throw herself at him, recapture his lips, and chase away any image he had of her polishing sneakers. As if! She threw them in the laundry with her whites.

But throwing herself at him would truly complicate a relationship she had just realized was going to last a long, long time.

Numbly, she dragged her suitcase into the bathroom and changed from her pajamas. She thought it was just a little pathetic how hard she tried to look nice. She packed all her things and he took her suitcase as if it weighed nothing and tossed it in the back of his truck.

''You paid up here?'' he asked.

She nodded.

"You might as well leave your car out at my place," he said. "It'll keep poor old Rufus from wondering why it's still here and you're gone."

"But I'll need my car. Once I'm home."

"I thought maybe we'd just pick Jed up, and head on back here. I could get to know him on my own turf."

"What makes you think I can just put my life on hold like that?"

"Kind of got you figured for a schoolmarm," he said, sending her a sidelong look. "I bet you have the whole summer off."

"I am not a *schoolmarm*. What a ridiculous term." She could not believe he had pegged her so easily.

"But you do teach school, don't you?"

How she would love to tell him she was a belly dancer at the Fruit-of-the-Loin Club in downtown Regina! How she would love to tell him her work for the government was top secret, and she couldn't discuss it with him.

But of course, lies did not come easily to her. "I teach grade five," she admitted coolly. "At a private school."

He nodded an annoying just-as-I-thought nod.

He opened her car door, on the driver's side and she slid in behind the wheel. He looked down at her. "Don't try anything," he said. "Just straight out to my place. I'll be right behind you."

How she would have loved to try something! A high-speed chase through the streets of Dancer, a swift right-hand turn onto the prairie, just like in the movies. That would erase that smug certainty from him that she was somehow boring and predictable and that those were bad things.

Had she actually agreed to bring Jed back here?

She started her car and drove carefully out to J.D.'s place. She waited while he got out of the truck and then started asking all the questions she had been thinking of as she drove.

"How long are you thinking Jed should come visit? And where are we going to stay? And what are we going to tell him?"

He held up a hand. "Lady, one thing at a time. First I need a pair of socks. Then I can start mapping out a careful course for the rest of my life."

A half hour later she was sitting beside him in his truck, that horrible smelly dog right on top of her feet.

She had protested the dog, but J.D. had just reminded her, with infuriating calm, that he was in control now, and the dog was nonnegotiable.

He was driving silently through the darkness, his face a mask that told her nothing about what he was thinking. He certainly did not seem to be mapping out the rest of his life.

The dog tried to get up on the seat beside her. She pushed him down, and he looked at her sadly.

She meant to stay wide-awake. She ordered herself to be alert, to maintain some modicum of control over this bizarre situation.

But the highway unfolding endlessly into darkness made her eyes heavy. She awoke once to find the dog had climbed onto the seat after all, and had stretched out, his big smelly head on her lap. When he noticed she was awake, he nudged her hand, hoping to be petted.

"Ugh," she told him.

"For a schoolmarm," J.D. said, "you have a very limited vocabulary."

She gave him her best look of schoolmarmish displeasure, which seemed to faze him not one little bit. The dog nudged her again, and she gave him a tiny, reluctant pat on the head before she went back to sleep.

It occurred to her, just before she slept, that her life was now well and truly out of her control.

And that she had survived. She was alive. Her world had not disintegrated into a billion pieces that she would never be able to put back together.

"Yet," she mumbled.

J.D. glanced at the woman sleeping on the seat of the truck beside him. Had she muttered something in her sleep, anxious about the order of her world?

"Anything would be an improvement," J.D. said, glaring at her. She'd put her hair back up in the bun, and her sneakers were practically glowing in the dark.

Beauford had his head on her lap, oblivious to her dislike for him, or maybe forgiving of it. It was said a dog could see right through a facade, right to the heart. Beauford seemed to have decided Miss High-and-Mighty had a good heart.

Her head had fallen sideways against the window, and her mouth was slightly open. A sputtering little snore, that would have embarrassed the hell out of her, came out of her.

Even in her sleep, he could not help but notice she looked worried, her forehead all puckered up, her hands in fists on her lap.

Well, he was just a little worried himself, not that he intended for her to see it. His life had just been totally upended. Totally.

Outside the truck a splendid dawn—pink and fiery orange and red and yellow—painted the prairie landscape in magnificence.

Up until the very moment she had confirmed it, there had been the slimmest chance J.D. had been wrong about the kid. Up until that moment it had remained a possibility that he was caught in some middle-of-the-night dementia, taking wild stabs in the dark. Though his heart had reached for the truth, and found it, he was unprepared for it. He had a child. The knowledge staggered him, a blow from a heavyweight.

A boy. He had a son, who had been named after him. A child who had walked his first steps without him, and spoken his first words without him, who had been without the protection and care of his father.

Despite believing Tally that her sister had been ill, he could not quell his sense of betrayal. Every missed birthday was a betrayal. Every missed milestone—first tooth, first steps, first words, first snowflakes—a betrayal. Every missed visit with Santa Claus, every missed Easter egg hunt, a betrayal.

For a man who had made a vow of being a bachelor for the rest of his life, it occurred to him he was not unhappy about the boy. Not at all.

Maybe because he could have the best of both worlds— a son, without the complication of the kind of family Tally was so hell-bent on finding. He made a mental note to call a lawyer to find out what his rights and responsibilities concerning his son were, though he was pretty sure if he listened to his heart, he'd get the less complicated version.

He glanced again at the sleeping woman. You'd think she'd have the good sense to be as disillusioned about families as he was. He suspected that hair, tortured into the neat bun, and that pucker in her brow had a lot to do with growing up in the shadow of her sister.

His own truth was that he had been disillusioned about the fairer sex long before Elana's first betrayal, never mind this more recent one.

His own life held shadows. His mother had never been

happy in Dancer. She had always conveniently blamed her unhappiness on J.D. and his father. He'd grown up listening to her litany of might-have-beens, should-have-beens. If not for them, she claimed, she would be sun-bathing in Saint-Tropez and skiing at Steamboat, surfing the wild North shore of Oahu. If not for the family that had tied her down she might have had a life of excitement and accomplishment and adventure, not a life of cooking and cleaning and driving to peewee hockey games.

She had, mercifully, left when J.D. was thirteen. He remembered his father and enjoying contentment in their simple house, finally. For awhile, she'd kept in touch, but she had seemed as unhappy as ever even with no one to blame it on.

Looking back as an adult, he could see the instability of his mother's nature, but at the time all that unhappiness had seemed like it was his fault.

Was it that, at some unconscious level, that had attracted him to Elana? Had he been trying to win the love of a woman, who just like his mother, was incapable of giving it? Had he been trying to fix a wound from his childhood?

He hated psychobabble. It was part of the membership agreement for the A.G.M.N.W.N. Club to boycott both Dr. Phil and Oprah. J. D. Turner was not given to intro-spection, nor the uncomfortable probing of his own mind. He put this unusual drifting now down to the fact he hadn't been up all night for a long, long time. It was making his mind go places he generally did not allow it to go. Snorting at himself in derision, he put on a tape. Country music. Some guy sang a great story song about going to prison, over a woman who done him wrong, and the tracking dog getting him out.

Beauford sighed happily, whined at all the right places.

Tally stretched and woke up, slowly. It was things like that—watching a woman come awake—that could make a man regret the road not taken.

There was a softness about her in those waking moments that could make a man look at the hardness of his life with faint regret.

"Where are we?" she asked. She tried to dislodge Beauford's head from her lap, but he sank deeper, rolling his eyes pleadingly upward at her. She scowled at the dog but gave up without a decent fight. J.D. wondered if that was her modus operandi—appear uptight and cool—to hide that scorching warmth he had tasted in her kisses, to hide the delicate softness he had sensed in her waking moments.

J.D. told her where they were. "I'll stop for breakfast and a coffee at the next town."

Tally sighed and looked at the window. She took a deep breath, as if gathering courage and then said, "I'm sorry you didn't know about him sooner."

He glanced at her. Had his thoughts, his sense of loss and betrayal, somehow etched themselves in his face, for her to see?

"Elana always said she didn't know who the father was," Tally continued. "I had no reason to believe that wasn't true. She did really wild things, when she was up. She couldn't help herself."

He tried not to flinch. He had been one of the "wild things" Elana did. He had been sucked into the whirlwind of a baffling illness, and he had never suspected.

"I started to sort through Elana's things a couple of months ago. I found the picture. When I read the back of it, I knew you were my nephew's father. Biological father. I've been debating what to do ever since then.

"I thought you had a right to know. It seemed so unfair

to me that you didn't know. It wasn't your fault Elana was sick. But I also thought I should find out what kind of person you were before I even considered introducing you to Jed's life.''

"A lot of women would have put that picture right back in the box." He gave her that, grudgingly.

"A lot of men wouldn't care if they'd left a kid somewhere along the way. Wouldn't want to know. So, that seemed like step one to me. To find that out about you first."

"Tell me about him," he said. "Tell me about my son. Everything. From the day he was born."

"I have a picture."

He nearly threw Beauford onto the floor he pulled over to the shoulder so fast. "Let's see."

She rummaged around in that big purse she had hit him with and finally came out with a picture.

J.D. took it. It was a professional shot. A little boy sat on a stool, his hands folded neatly in his lap, his legs crossed. He was wearing a plaid shirt, suspenders, a goofy-looking bow tie. His dark hair had been slicked back, and his expression was very solemn as he gazed at the camera. He was pudgy-cheeked, and dark-eyed. His eyelashes were thick and black and tangled as a chimney brush.

J.D. traced the lines of his son's face. "I looked like this at this age," he murmured. "I have almost this identical picture somewhere. Only of me. No bow tie, thank God."

"There's nothing wrong with bow ties!" she said, way too defensively, and then seemed to realize she had overreacted. "When I saw your picture in Elana's things, I really didn't have any doubt. Those beautiful brown eyes."

She caught herself and blushed.

So, Tally Smith thought he had beautiful eyes. For some reason he liked that nearly as much as he liked looking at this picture of his boy.

How complicated his life had become in the past twenty-four hours.

He handed her back the picture and pulled back onto the highway. "How old is he in that picture?"

"It was taken a few months ago. At a Sears portrait day. You know. Six ninety-nine for all the pictures you want."

He didn't know. Because he had missed all those things that parents knew. Because of Elana.

He suspected that all her life, Tally Smith had been trying to fix her sister's mistakes.

But this one was too big for her.

"So now tell me everything," he ordered gruffly, "from the second he was born."

She gathered her thoughts, and then began. "He was born at 6:02 in the morning on April 10. You know how you picture babies coming out yelling and screaming? Not him. A little Buddha, right from the start."

Out of the corner of his eye, he saw some finely held tension in her let go as she talked about the boy. Despite the polished running shoes, and her dreams of a neat and tidy house, J.D. heard in her voice the love for that child, and knew, for all the stupid mistakes she was making, she was good for his son.

"Elana would kind of come and go," she said, "but I was always there."

Unsaid, he heard, *picking up the pieces.*

Tally talked about the kind of baby Jed had been. About buying him that little tiny bunny outfit for his first Easter. About giving him a mashed banana for his first real food.

She talked about the photocopy of his hand she had taken on the school copier, and about his love-hate relationship with a cat named Bitsy-Mitsy.

"He loves her, the cat hates him."

In a way he'd been Tally's baby right from the start. Elana there, and then gone, and then back, and then in the hospital. Tally had always been Jed's touchstone, his rock, his safe place.

She talked, and talked, and yet he could not hear enough. J.D. wanted to hear it all.

He wanted to hear about the crayon Jed had eaten, and the encounter with dog poop. He leaned forward eagerly when she told him about the little fishing rod she'd gotten him, and the baseball bat.

He realized that Tally was going to be a darn good mom for his son once he got her straightened out about a few things. Her world was just a little too well-ordered.

"Tell me a little about this guy you are going to marry," he said.

"Oh, Herbert's a lovely man. He owns the hardware store in Dogwood Hollow."

Lovely was such a generic term. And not exactly one J.D. could feel enthused about in terms of the man who would be helping to raise his son.

"What does lovely entail exactly?" J.D. asked.

"Oh, you know."

"I don't."

She seemed very uncomfortable. "Well, as I said, he has the hardware store, so he's very prosperous and stable."

Is that what he wanted his son learning about relationships? That prosperous and stable counted more than passionate and loving?

"Herbert has a heritage home. And stainless steel appliances in his kitchen. Bitsy-Mitsy is his cat."

J.D. didn't like it one little bit that she was cataloguing Herbert's belongings instead of his character. She didn't seem superficial so he had to assume, after the pain of loving her sister, Tally Smith was probably afraid to trust her heart.

"How does he feel about Jed?"

"He adores him!" she said, way too quickly.

J.D. took that to mean his son was tolerated. *Tolerated.*

"How does he show he *adores* him?" he asked.

"You should see the collection of Tonka trucks he's brought him from the hardware store."

Great. More stuff.

As the miles slipped by and she rattled on about Herbert, J.D. felt his mission was becoming clearer by the second. It was his sacred duty, his obligation to his son, to tilt her world right on its axis.

He was pretty sure it was going to be just about the most fun he'd ever had.

Chapter Four

Dogwood Hollow surprised J.D. by being quite a bit larger than Dancer. It actually had traffic lights, a small shopping mall and several office and apartment buildings.

They had been six hours together in his truck, and J.D. was pleased to see he was having a positive effect on her already. Tally Smith was looking quite rumpled. Her blouse was wrinkled, her slacks had dog hair on them, her hair was falling messily from the bun and her lipstick had worn off. Already she was a different woman than the pressed, perfectly turned out Miss Priss she had been yesterday.

And he'd had her in his power less than a full day! In no time he would be able to show her what a woman should know in order to raise his son.

"You look good," he told her gruffly, the opening maneuver of the mission. He needed to encourage this hair-let-down look and attitude.

She had found a book somewhere in that gigantic bag of hers, and though she had folded the cover over so he couldn't see it, she hadn't been quite fast enough. Just as he'd suspected a woman in a period costume that showed a great deal of breast had been running from a dark and sinister-looking castle. Tally looked up from her book reluctantly, and focused on him with a frown.

"What?"

Here she was in the cab of the truck with a real live man, and she had her attention riveted on the fictional item? He was slightly offended by that, though of course he had browbeaten her. There was also the possibility he smelled like a real live man at the moment.

As gallantly as he could, he said, "You look nice right now."

She gaped at him, then turned away, pressed her face to the window and caught a glimpse of her reflection in the side view mirror. She grimaced then looked down at herself, tried to straighten her blouse, and picked a few stray hairs off her slacks.

"I suppose you think you're funny," she said in a tone that went much better with her old self.

"Not at all. You do look better. More real. Relaxed. You know?"

"I do not," she said and returned her interest to the book.

His gallantry had been rejected! The opening maneuver abandoned, he snapped, "I feel sorry for the kids you teach. You're as uptight and tense as a hen in a coyote den. One frog in the desk drawer and they're probably writing lines for life."

"My students would not dare put a frog in my desk drawer," she said, not looking up from the book, and then, "At least I'm a good-looking hen in the coyote den, according to you."

It wasn't good enough to reject his gallantry. Oh, no,

she had to throw it back in his face. "You make me wish to be in grade five again."

"You mean you aren't?" she said with artificial sweetness.

"See what I mean? Uptight."

He watched out of the corner of his eye as her lips pursed up in a precise underscore of what he had just said about her being uptight. At least he was getting to her!

Her voice very measured, she said, "I have been forced from my bed in the middle of the night, had a stinky dog drooling on my lap for six hours, been subjected to your driving, which is borderline reckless, and I'm uptight? I think I should be nominated for sainthood."

"Same thing," he said, "as uptight. So, you're nominated. Saint Tally of Dogwood Hollow. And I do not drive recklessly. I drive fast because I know *exactly* the capabilities of my vehicles and myself. Besides, with a bona fide saint on board, what do I have to worry about?"

"You were incorrigible in school, weren't you?"

"That's right," he said happily. "Incorrigible. Incorrigible and the Saint. It would make a good title for a book, wouldn't it?"

"And that tells me everything I need to know about your reading material."

"You're commenting on my reading material? What are you reading? The Duchess and the Duke Do It at Dorchester?"

"As it happens this is an excellent study of life in the Victorian era. The research is impeccable."

"Well, if people really wore dresses like that one on the cover, I envy the duke. There must have been surprises falling out all over the place."

She sniffed regally, arched a snobby eyebrow at him, and returned to her book. The attitude was in contrast to her appearance. He decided he liked how she looked because she looked amazingly as if she'd just tumbled out of bed after a wild romp. He decided not to share that with her.

His urge to stop the truck and kiss her until she went crazy was strong. He told himself, not without righteousness, kissing her was probably going to be par for the course, part of what the woman who was going to be raising his son needed to know.

That you didn't settle in life. You didn't settle for stainless steel appliances instead of wild, hungry nights of endless passion.

But even as he had that thought, it occurred to him, uncomfortably, that maybe he had settled himself. Hadn't he chosen a life that was safe and predictable instead of spontaneous and daring? Where was the passion in his life? Clyde Walters's '72 Mustang hardly counted.

"Well, maybe we're both going to learn a little something," he muttered.

"Pardon?"

"Can't you say 'what?' like normal people?"

"Are you a normal person?"

"Yep."

"Then, no I can't."

Having successfully diverted her so he didn't have to share the life lesson he was learning, he tried to return his attention just to the road. But the question had been asked now. Wasn't he settling, too?

"No!" he said out loud.

She cast him an apprehensive look.

"I'm tired," he snapped. And that explained everything, really. He decided the all-night drive was warping his thinking. His life was not safe and predictable. He had fun. He took apart old cars and put his feet up on the coffee table. He sang in the shower. He was the rarest of things. A free man. He was the charter member of the A.G.M.N.W.N. Club. What more could he ask for?

Her scent—warm and lemony—chose that moment to fill up the whole truck and wrap itself around his overly tired senses.

He pulled himself up short. He told himself he was a soldier, with a mission. Save his son from her uptight world.

Period. Emotional involvement was unnecessary. No, downright dangerous. Lemon scent should be outlawed.

"This is where we live."

He pulled over and eyed her home critically, still a soldier, sizing up his mission. It was a nice apartment building—two stories high, freshly painted, big balconies, nice landscaping. J.D. was aware he couldn't stand it that his son lived here.

"Come on, Beau, out."

"Oh, he can't come in."

J.D. narrowed his eyes at her. She really couldn't get it through her head that she was not calling the shots.

"What? Someone will call the dog squad if he enters the apartment?"

"It's just not allowed."

There was lesson number two. Right after he convinced her you didn't settle in life, he was going to have to teach her too many rules were damaging to a small boy's spirit. Actually, to anyone with any spirit. Imagine a world with so many rules that a perfectly well-mannered, one hundred percent housebroken animal would be banned from a building!

"Tell you what," he said, calling Beau to his side, "Let's live dangerously."

She glared at him, and muttered, "What do you think

we've been doing for the last six hours with you at the wheel?''

But he ignored her and took her suitcase out of the back of the truck. "Lead on," he said.

Her jaw locked stubbornly, her fists clenched at her sides, she marched toward the front door. Tut-tut. The tension!

There were neat flower beds lining the sidewalk, which J.D. hated because a small child probably got in trouble for trampling them. It looked like that kind of place. He spotted a hand-printed Keep Off The Grass sign on the manicured lawn, and sighed.

The door was locked. She had to punch a code to get in.

"Crime rate high here?" he asked conversationally, but he didn't feel conversational. If his son was living in a high crime area, that was it. Mission revised immediately. Both of them, Tally and Jed, stuffed in his truck and taken to Dancer never to be returned.

Which is about the scariest thought J. D. Turner had ever had. Tally Smith in Dancer? Permanently?

A man could run a mission when it had a time limit on it. He couldn't resist the temptations of lemon scent forever.

"Of course it's not a high crime area," she said, "but there are places in the world where people lock their doors."

He knew that. He just didn't think his son should live in one of them.

She led him into a nice foyer. It had a light-colored leather couch that looked like it marked easily, a carpet that looked like it had come from the bazaar in Istanbul and a four foot glass vase sprouting peacock feathers. The vase, aside from looking impractical and plain silly, looked highly breakable. J.D. bet a kid would probably get chewed out for throwing a ball or running or having muddy feet.

Beauford sniffed a large potted tree and instantly forgot he was perfectly trained and one hundred percent house-broken.

"No," J.D. cried as Beauford lifted his leg. The dog dropped his leg and gave him a hurt look. "Well, who can blame him," J.D. defended against Tally's I-told-you-so-look. "It confused him to find a tree inside."

The tree was big enough for a small boy to climb, but J.D. bet that wasn't allowed either.

Beauford gave him another hurt look and shuffled along with them to the elevator. He whined when they got inside and the door slid closed.

"I don't like them much myself," he muttered.

"Don't like what?" she asked.

At the risk of appearing like a complete hick, he said tightly, "Elevators. Too confined. Don't like the way they make my stomach feel."

If she laughed, he could commence with the kissing lesson right now, and wipe that look of smug superiority right off her face.

But she didn't laugh, and in fact the tight look left her face.

Sympathy replaced it!

He glared at her until she looked away. When the elevator door opened Beauford rushed off in a panic, nearly knocking over an elderly woman in a pink jogging suit who was punching the button impatiently.

"Well, I never," she said indignantly.

A building full of uptight people!

"Ms. Smith, really," Pink Jogger said, "there are no dogs allowed in the building, as you well know."

Tally shot him a baleful look, and he took a deep breath, deliberately increasing his chest size. He disliked the old bat on principle. He was willing to bet she used that same tone of voice on *his* boy. No running. Too much noise. Don't play. He bet she was responsible for that sign on the grass.

"Undercover," he snarled, and then gestured at the dog, "K-9."

"Oh," she said. "Oh my." She studied him with wide-eyed and ghoulish curiosity, got on the elevator and reluctantly let the door slide shut.

Tally's mouth was very tight. "She believed you. How could you do that?" she snarled. "I have to live in this building. I'll be the talk of the laundry room that I was escorted in by the police and a drug-sniffing dog."

"After all the rumors you've started about my life? We're not anywhere close to being even," he said dryly. "Besides, I'm not responsible for what she thinks. I never told her I was a cop. That would be illegal."

"You did so. You said—"

She stopped and remembered what he had said.

He smiled at her. "Undercover," he confirmed. "And I was under covers not so long ago. Actually, I'm not so bad under covers."

She blushed an unbecoming shade of beet-red that he nevertheless found he liked. All part of the plan. Un-uptight her. Shock her a bit. If she pictured him under covers, so much the better.

Unfortunately, the picture that formed seemed to be in his own mind. Of a wild and hungry night of endless passion with her.

Instructive only.

He gulped and said, his voice hoarse, "And, of course,

Beauford is a canine. There is absolutely no doubt about that.''

He noticed something very interesting. The tightness around her mouth wasn't because she was angry. It was because she was trying not to laugh.

God, what a job it was going to be to teach this woman to let go!

She turned quickly away from him and led him down the hall. She knocked on the door and then inserted her key. But before she had turned the bolt completely, he heard wild scrabbling on the other side of the door, and then it was flung open, and her knees were attacked by a pint-size quarterback.

She laughed then.

It was a rich and joyous sound that almost distracted him from the miracle that was his son. Almost.

The boy was beautiful, sturdy and strong. Other fathers had their moment in the delivery room. This was J.D.'s moment and nothing in his life experience had prepared him for the glorious reality of his son. J.D. noticed his own features stamped strongly on the child's face. He noticed Jed's coloring, the brilliance of his smile, the light that shone deep and bright in mischievous brown eyes.

J.D. felt astounded by this miracle. His child, his flesh and blood, so real that he could almost sense energy and life exuding from Jed in powerful waves.

Tally hooted, an un-Tally-like sound, and lifted Jed up with surprising strength. She wrapped her arms around the child and hugged hard. After a moment, Jed captured her face between his two chubby hands and smothered her in kisses while she pretended to try and evade him and laughed helplessly.

In that moment, J.D. had a stunning picture of who

Tally really was, and it was so bright and so beautiful it nearly blinded him.

For a moment his mission faltered. She did not look like a woman who needed any help from him.

When it felt like he might be sucked into the vortex of her energy, he looked away from her, and noticed another woman, standing in the shadow of the apartment hallway.

His reaction was one of grave sympathy for the male world. There was yet another gorgeous Smith sister, that same blond hair, fine bone structure and amazing eyes.

"I'm Kailey," she said, coming forward. He knew immediately she was shy...and scared. Tally had called and let her know they were coming, but he suddenly saw that tilting a world on its axis was a very grave undertaking.

He considered himself something of a moron when it came to sensitivity but he knew he had to let Kailey know her world was going to be okay, that he wasn't going to pull Jed out from under them or anything like that.

That he was just going to retrain her sister.

Since he couldn't think of the words, he took her hand, and gave it a reassuring squeeze, and looked long and hard right into her eyes. Considering how gorgeous she was, and that she was a Smith, the handshake proved somewhat surprising.

He did not have that sensation of having been shocked that he got when he touched Tally. In fact, shaking hands with Kailey had a rather sisterly feel to it.

Kailey smiled, suddenly, quickly, and the fear dissolved in her eyes.

Jed had nestled into Tally's shoulder and was now peeking at J.D. Jed's thumb found its way to his mouth and he took a couple of happy slurps on it.

Was four too old for thumb-sucking? For the first time it occurred to J.D. this fatherhood stuff might be a little more complicated than setting Tally on the right track. How did he know what the right track was? No wonder she read books!

"Jed, this is J.D. He's a friend of mine," Tally said, just as they had agreed.

Jed scrutinized him carefully, and popped his thumb out of his mouth. He smiled tentatively. "Hawo."

His son liked him! J.D. could feel his heart swelling inside his chest. His son—

The reunion was cut short when Jed suddenly spotted the dog. With a cry of surprised delight he wriggled down out of Tally's arms and squatted in front of Beauford.

"Puppy," he said reverently.

Beauford and Jed regarded each other with grave interest, and then they both sighed, the very same happy, contented soul-deep sound.

"A dog lover," J.D. breathed with satisfaction.

"It must be genetic," Tally said woefully.

Jed threw his arms around Beauford's solid neck and kissed him as thoroughly as he had his aunt.

Beauford's stumpy tail thumped happily. He drooled with delight.

"Jed," Tally said. "Don't kiss his mouth. Dirty. Germs."

Lesson three, J.D. thought. *Germs are rarely deadly. Dog kisses are one of life's delights.* But maybe, now that he thought about it, only in a life that had become devoid of other kinds of kisses. He would have to give some more thought to lesson three, obviously.

Jed, thankfully, gave his aunt a look of injured disbelief. Beauford, insulted, shook loose the child, and ambled uninvited into the apartment with the little boy hard on his heels.

The apartment reminded J.D. of how crucial his mission was. It was just no place for a child.

Though it was a nice enough apartment, it was tiny and distinctly feminine. There was a disconcerting amount of pink in the decorating, and there were all kinds of little breakable trinkets around that would not be conducive to roughhousing.

The balcony, visible through a large sliding window, had a tricycle on it. The thought of his son riding his trike around that limited space made J.D. think, painfully, of a baby tiger prowling a cage.

Toys, instead of being in a happy heap in the middle of the floor, were neatly organized in a stacking wall unit. A single large yellow truck toy was out on the floor.

It looked like a desperate place for a little kid to try and grow up, though at least the toy wasn't a doll.

''I'm going to be evicted,'' Tally said sorrowfully when the dog and the boy romped noisily out of the room, down the hall and back again. It confirmed J.D.'s worst suspicion that good, healthy, wholesome noise would be frowned upon in a place like this.

J.D. refrained from saying he could think of worse things than her being evicted only because he couldn't help but notice her eyes were soft as she watched the boy tumble across the living room floor with the dog.

He sat down carefully on the couch. It looked brand-new and like it might be easily damaged by the weight of a real man. It was light beige, which he thought was a dumb color to pick if you were raising a small boy. He could see two bedrooms off the living room, the doors to both ajar.

Jed's room was obvious, a cheerful space, decorated in bright primary colors.

Hers, next door, was done in virginal whites.

Virginal.

He was way, way too tired because he actually entertained the notion of asking her. He almost laughed out loud picturing how she would react to that question. *Hey, Tally, you a virgin?* Thankfully, the dog raced by, barking, Jed hot on his heels, squealing with childish laughter. J.D. had to remember not to shake her up too badly. If he managed to alienate her completely his mission would fail.

As he watched his son and Beauford, J.D. could feel a smile inside himself that was entirely different from any smile he had ever smiled before.

His son was a delight in every way. Jed was lively and intense, one hundred per cent boy. Tally had wanted a father for her nephew, and she had found one. Of course, she had to be dissuaded from the nuclear family nonsense she had attached to the title "daddy". J.D. knew he could be a very effective parent on a long-distance basis. He would phone. He would send cards and letters and gifts. They would travel back and forth. He would come here to visit, and Jed could come see him. J.D. could picture summer afternoons, hand in hand with his son, heading to the fishing hole, the dog trailing behind them. J.D.'s future suddenly glowed with the shining promise of snowball fights and snow forts, building go-carts, breaking in the leather of brand-new ball gloves, the crack of the bat hitting the ball.

Something in him relaxed the way it had not relaxed in a long, long time.

The last thing he remembered hearing was Tally moaning that her downstairs neighbor was going to start pounding on the ceiling in a minute.

He muttered something about dealing with the neighbor if that happened, and then he was gone.

"He's so nice," Kailey whispered to Tally as they sat at the kitchen table sipping tea. The dog was asleep under the table, and Jed was asleep right on top of him.

"I hope he doesn't have fleas," Tally said.

"J.D.?" Kailey asked with horror.

"Of course not. The beast under the table." Three males in her house for the first time in history and all of them fast asleep. And all of them snored.

It seemed entirely unfair to her that she knew J. D. Turner snored and she had no idea if Herbert Henley did or not.

"I was talking about J.D., but the dog's nice, too," Kailey said.

Kailey thought everyone and everything was nice. How she had ended up with one sister so wild and one so hopelessly naive was one of life's unexplainable mysteries to Tally.

"You've exchanged names and a handshake with J. D. Turner," Tally reminded her. "That's hardly a reference from his minister."

"I'm sure you've got all those angles covered," Kailey said. "He wouldn't be here right now if you hadn't liked what you found out about him."

That wasn't exactly true but there was no sense Kailey knowing the humiliating truth that he had wrestled the upper hand from Tally with disgusting ease.

"He's also," Kailey leaned close across the kitchen table and lowered her voice even further, "very cute."

Tally didn't think cute quite said it, but she decided not to argue that point either. That would only tell her sister she'd been paying attention. But J. D. Turner cute? Awesome. Magnificent. Powerful. Intimidating.

Of course, six hours in the cab of a truck, what else was there to notice? Besides Beauford? And a prairie landscape that repeated itself endlessly? And that the hero of the book she was reading seemed disappointingly insipid?

She knew now, how J.D.'s eyelashes were so thick they cast shadows on his cheeks. She knew his whiskers came in fast, dark and vigorous. She knew he drummed the steering wheel with one hand, and that his knuckles had a faint dusting of springy dark hair growing from them. She knew the large muscle of his thigh leapt to life every time he changed gears and looked like steel as they pressed into the faded fabric of his jeans. She knew his biceps flexed and bulged at the least hint of motion, like flipping the tape in his stereo.

He hummed to songs he liked, but he never burst into song the way he had that first night when she had caught him in the shower. He swore at other drivers. He threw his trash on the floor. She knew how J. D. Turner smelled, for God's sake. Like a real man. Like fresh-turned soil. She imagined his smell was that of the sun on ripening wheat. Clean and strong and pure. It was the faint scent of things brand-new springing from the earth, reaching toward the sun, ripening.

It seemed to her she knew far too much about J. D. Turner, far more than she had ever set out to know. She had set out to know if he was a decent man. Instead she knew his scent and the sweep of his lashes. The hard set of his thigh muscle. The quirk of his mouth. The taste of his lips.

"Are you blushing?" Kailey asked.

"Of course not!" But just in case she was, Tally tried,

desperately, to recall if Herbert had a scent. If she conjured hard enough, she could imagine he smelled faintly of his hardware store—of chemicals and boxes and paint and of things gathering dust on back shelves.

"So, you couldn't say on the phone, but why is he here?"

"As soon as he found out he had a son, he just piled me into the truck. He wants to take Jed and I back to Dancer with him for a week or two. To get to know Jed."

"He's not going to try and take him is he?" Kailey asked, sudden fear making her eyes huge.

"Of course not. I have the situation under control." Okay, J. D. Turner didn't know that yet, but he soon would.

"You should marry him," Kailey said dreamily.

"There is more to marriage than a man being cute!" She held up her ring finger, reminding her sister—and maybe herself—that she was taken. That she didn't even have to entertain the disturbing notion of marrying J. D. Turner, because she was marrying someone else.

"That may be," Kailey said, a stubborn note in her voice, "but there is also more to marriage than a stainless steel stovetop. Which I think is ugly, not that you asked."

"Good for you," J. D. said. He stood in the doorway looking rumpled and annoyingly adorable. "Isn't this stainless steel on the rim of the stove here?"

Tally nodded warily. She could only hope he had not heard the part about her sister marrying her off to him, or the part that he was cute.

J.D. pressed his finger against the burner rim on the stove, studied the spot, then shook his head with disgust. "Just as I thought," he said. "Fingerprints. Come and see if you don't believe me."

"And your discovery would interest me for what reason?"

"Little boys leave fingerprints."

"Not if they have clean hands," she said acidly.

"Which, hopefully, is hardly ever. No, I don't think stainless steel appliances go with children."

"I don't think I asked you."

"Tally," Kailey said. "He may have a point."

Oh! Traitor. Her own flesh and blood.

"I see," Tally said stiffly, "that I confided my enjoyment in those appliances to the wrong people. Can't either of you see it's not the appliances? It's about what they represent?"

Kailey and J.D. exchanged baffled looks.

"Okay," he finally said. "What do they represent?"

"Family dinners," Tally said. "Tradition."

They both still looked blank, so she rushed on, full of feeling, "The appliances represent a man who actually likes domestic things. Who cares about his surroundings. Who is willing to spend his money on unexciting things, but things that matter just the same. He could have had tickets to the Super Bowl—"

"He could have? Really?" J.D. asked.

"But he wanted something permanent. Something that lasted. Something of value."

"He could have framed the program," J.D. said with disgust. "Kept his ticket stubs in a jar on the fireplace."

"You don't get it," Tally said.

"Sure I do. You're planning to marry a man who is unfit to raise my son. Not that I would dream of stopping you. But you need to know a few things. First."

"What kind of things?" she asked suspiciously.

"I'll show you when we get back to Dancer. Boy stuff. You need to know some boy stuff. Since Herbie doesn't."

"He doesn't like being called Herbie," Tally said, her voice tight. "And I'm sure he knows all kinds of boy stuff. He owns a hardware store. That means lawn mowers. Pipe wrenches. Different sized nails. What could be more boy stuff than that?"

J.D. snorted. "He bought a stove instead of a Super Bowl ticket. This is worse than I could have imagined."

"Well, I think it's terribly exciting that the three of you are going to Dancer," Kailey said, confirming her role as a complete traitor. Her sister, Kailey Benedict Arnold.

"You don't know Dancer," J.D. corrected her gently. "It's not exactly exciting."

Finally, something they could agree on, though Tally didn't appreciate him one bit more. What was that nice tone of voice he used on his sister, but not on her?

"No, Dancer is not exciting," J.D. continued, "but it's spacious and open. You can still set off firecrackers on Main Street, and shoot gophers on the prairie. The general store still gives jawbreakers to little kids, and you can find the rattles off snakes on a lucky day."

"Oh," Kailey breathed, with perfect understanding, "boy stuff."

Tally glared at her, hoping she would pick up the traitor message, but she didn't. Kailey and J.D. were beaming at each other as if they were members of an exclusive secret society.

"Exactly," he said.

"Jed is too young to shoot gophers," Tally said, "not that I would let him if he was old enough. It's disgusting. Shooting small furry creatures is despicable. I won't even discuss snakes, except to let you know all parts of them would be crawling with germs. And jawbreakers are a choking hazard to children under five. I read it in a book."

J.D. was smiling at her, so indulgently it made her see red.

"Your whole problem, Tally—"

How dare he insinuate she have a problem?

"—is that you have done far too much reading, and far too little living."

She folded her arms over her chest. "And you are going to fix my problem?" she said.

He missed her sarcasm entirely. "Exactly," he said happily, as if she was a dull child who had just gotten it. "I better work on Herbie's while I'm here, too. When can I meet him?"

Chapter Five

Tally stared at J.D., aghast. He was going to fix her problems? She didn't have any problems. He should look around. There was no engine ripped to bits on her kitchen counter! She did not flaunt herself by answering the door in a bath towel! Or flaunt the rules by marching a dog through a building where animals were specifically prohibited.

And as if insinuating she had problems was not bad enough, J. D. Turner was also going to pick on Herbert? Presumably J.D. had reached the conclusion of Herbert having problems based on Herbert's extremely mature and sensitive decision to forego a Super Bowl ticket in favor of investing in appliances.

The unadulterated ego of J. D. Turner! Tally had always known this about good-looking men. They were just too sure of themselves, cocky to the point of being offensive. No wonder she had chosen Herbert.

After opening her mouth several times, and no sound

coming out, she finally found her voice. "Why you smug, sanctimonious…so-and-so."

J.D. grinned at her sister, all easygoing charm. "She almost called me an S.O.B., didn't she?"

Kailey Benedict Arnold nodded in solemn agreement. "I think so."

"That's good. I think it would be good for Jed if she relaxed a bit. You know, if she wasn't so darn perfect, if she realized it was okay to be human. Lost her temper every now and then."

J.D. was talking to her sister about her as though she wasn't here!

She inserted herself back into the conversation. "Swearing in front of a child is being human? Then no thank you. And I do not lose my temper."

"Well, the child is sleeping," J.D. said. "You could probably let your guard down a wee bit. And you know, I think I detect a small edge in your voice right now."

"My guard is always up," she said, carefully modulating her tone.

"That's what I was afraid of."

"Quit talking about me as if I'm some big project you've undertaken, and get it out of your head that you are interviewing my fiancé. Herbert does not need any advice from you, nor do I!"

"I wouldn't dream of giving you advice," he said easily. "I'm just getting the lay of the land." He walked over to the phone on the counter, picked up the phone book from underneath it and flipped through to the yellow pages.

"Gee, imagine that. Only one Henley's Hardware Store in all of Dogwood Hollow."

"Don't you dare."

"What do you know? Henley's Hardware is Dogwood

Hollow's exclusive dealer in Airbeam stainless steel appliances. Hey, Tally, he got that fridge and stove at cost.''

He was dialing the number. He had the audacity to wink at her.

Tally could not believe this. All those years of dealing with her impossible sister and she had always handled every situation with the three *C*s: calm, compassion and composure. Every single one!

And here she was, leaping across the kitchen, trying to tear the phone out of the hands of a man who was holding it out of her reach and laughing at her as if she was an overly enthusiastic puppy.

"Herbert Henley please," J.D. said, holding Tally at arm's length with easy strength.

Kailey Benedict Arnold was bent over in her chair, holding her stomach, howling with laughter. If she wasn't careful she'd wake up Jed, not to mention the dead.

"Hi there, Herbert. My name's John David Turner. I'm a recent acquaintance of Tally Smith's. Did she happen to mention me to you? She didn't?''

Tally gave up trying to get the phone from him, folded her arms over her chest and squinted evilly at him. J. D. Turner was unintimidated by evil squints.

"She didn't tell you she chased me right down to Dancer, North Dakota?" he said, injecting amazement into his voice. "She told you what? Going away on school business?'' J.D. raised his eyebrows at her.

Kailey was on the floor, rolling around, tears spurting out of her eyes. Tally turned her gaze on her, but her sister was suddenly immune to the evil squint, too.

Tally added a foot tap to her pose. It was a stance that had quelled dozens of unruly schoolchildren.

But J.D. just waggled his eyebrows fiendishly at her.

"I'm Jed's dad. She found a picture of me in an old

photograph album of Elana's and figured it out. Clever girl, huh? You don't think she's a girl? Well, now I figure there's plenty of girl left in her. Anyway, the reason I'm calling is I understand that things are getting pretty serious between the two of you, and since you are going to be a person of consequence in my son's life, it seems only fair to me we should meet. I won't be able to be in Dogwood Hollow very long, so tonight would work.

"Your place? Well, I think that would be just fine. I'll just check with Tally." He put the phone down against his chest. "What do you think, Tally?"

What was wrong with this picture? He was acting like *they* were the couple. And it was his chest she'd seen, and his lips he'd kissed, and her world was going all wrong somehow and it was all his fault.

"I am not giving in to this manipulative behavior," she growled.

He smiled and put the phone back up to his ear. "She says she's busy, but I'm still game. Great. Meet you at eight. She'll tell me where to go, I'm sure."

He hung up the phone.

"You are not going to meet Herbert," she sputtered.

"Why? Are you ashamed of him?" He crossed his arms over his chest, and leaned his fanny against her countertop. Amusement burned through his dark eyes.

"No!" Though it crossed her mind, to her great shame, that she didn't think Herbert was going to stack up very well on J.D.'s scale. J.D. would probably stare at his bow tie, and judge his little tummy, and think because he wore glasses he was a wimp. "You have no right to barge into my life like this."

"Well, I hate to be the one to remind you, Tally, but it was really you who started the barging business. You conducted personal interviews about me all over Dancer.

Behind my back, I might add. At least all this is out in the open.''

"We are not going to Herbert's tonight," she said. She couldn't imagine a more awkward situation if she tried.

"Honey, you may not be going to Herbert's tonight, but I am. Actually, it might be better without you there. I'll stop at the liquor store and get a nice bottle of Canadian rye whiskey, loosen up his tongue and learn everything there is to know about you."

"That's despicable. And don't call me honey. I am not your honey. And Herbert does not know everything there is to know about me."

"Now that's a real shame because he should if anybody does. I mean if you're planning to get married and all."

He said that as if he doubted the seriousness of their wedding plans. Had Herbert said something to him?

"Does he know you wear lace bras?" J.D. said, with extreme casualness, the same tone he might have used if he said *does he know you drive a Nissan?*

She heard Kailey stop laughing long enough to gasp appreciatively.

"No, he does not!"

As soon as he grinned Tally knew she was being played by a master. He was trying to find out if she'd been intimate with Herbert. She actually felt herself blushing. She actually wondered why on earth he wanted to know, since he had made it so plain he was not interested in being part of the domestic bliss that would come from creating a perfect family for Jed.

She forced herself to come to her senses. She drew herself to her full height. Enough was enough. She was taking back the power position in her life and she was doing it right now. She couldn't think of a scenario more horrible than J.D. alone with Herbert prying all the details of their relationship from him.

Of course, she might have a different attitude if those details were a whole lot more interesting than they were.

"If you go and see Herbert without my approval," she said regally, "Jed and I will not be accompanying you back to Dancer."

Kailey gasped again.

J.D. went very still. Though his casual stance did not change, the laughter drained from his eyes, they narrowed dangerously and he regarded her with discomforting intensity.

"That's your big card, sweetheart. You want to play it so early in the game?"

"Don't call me sweetheart."

"Just answer the question."

"I mean it."

"Okay. I mean this. And I am saying it once, so you better hear me. I'm prepared to keep this all nice and friendly. I want to get to know my son, and all the people who are going to be major players in his life. And then I want you and I to reach a mutually agreeable decision about what my involvement in his life is going to be.

"I can tell you're a great mom to him and that you have a great support system." He nodded toward Kailey Benedict Arnold, who beamed at him. "I have no interest in changing that. I want to visit him, and I want to know what's going on in his life. Those seem like reasonable requests to me. Nothing that needs to involve a judge or lawyers.

"But," his voice softened dangerously, "if you ever try and keep me from doing what I think is in my son's best interests, the friendliness ends. And Tally Smith?"

He waited until she nodded, and she could have kicked herself when she did.

"You don't want me for an enemy."

His eyes were absolutely blazing. His mouth was a firm, uncompromising line. She could see a fine tension appear in the muscles of his folded arms. She realized it was true. She did not want him for an enemy.

And it seemed far too dangerous to have him for a friend.

He was in control again! Totally and completely.

"Humph," she said, with as much dignity as she could muster. She tilted her chin, turned on her heel and went into her bedroom and slammed the door. She pounded the pillow with her fists for a full five minutes she was so mad.

The temper tantrum astonished her! She was always the one in control. Always! It occurred to her he had had the upper hand for quite some time now.

And she was surviving. Tally Smith not being in control might not mean the end of the world after all.

With that strangely contented thought in her mind, she put her head back on her pillow and went to sleep. And when she got up, she knew she was going to Herbert's. Apparently so did Kailey.

Because the black strapless dress that Kailey had worn when Chris Palmer, Dogwood Hollow's mayor, had taken her to the opera in Winnipeg last year, was laid out carefully on the end of the bed.

A ridiculous dress to wear over to Herbert's. Tally assumed they were going for a cup of coffee and some imported cookies out of a tin. A swipe of lipstick, a pair of slacks, a blouse and a sweater would be fine.

Still, the dress was there. It wouldn't hurt to try it on, would it?

The dress slid on like a second skin. It fit like a second skin. Tally didn't remember it looking quite this *naughty* when Kailey had worn it.

She spun in front of the mirror, and admired her transformation. From schoolmarm to siren in the blink of an eye. The dress made her legs look longer, and her bust look fuller. The air on her naked shoulders made her feel sensuous, and the blackness of the dress made her eyes look smoldering.

What was Kailey thinking? She couldn't wear this dress over to Herbert's.

Still, it was kind of fun looking at herself in it. What had J.D. called her? Miss Control? Miss Schoolmarm?

Well, she didn't look like either now.

And suddenly she was damned tired of being dismissed. She was going to make them both—Herbert and J.D.— sit up and take notice tonight.

There was more than one way to gain control over a man.

She put her hand on her hip, batted her eyelashes and licked her lips. And then she smiled, a slow and sultry smile. Maybe J.D. was right. She needed to loosen up a bit.

When she emerged from the bedroom, a half hour later, she had done her hair, sweeping it up more softly than usual. She had put on darker lipstick than she normally wore, and enough mascara to feel she was peering out of her eyes through a mass of tangled spiders legs.

J.D. was roughhousing on the living room floor with Jed and Beauford. They had dog-piled him, and he was lying underneath them pretending he was completely pinned. The dog licked his face, and Jed was trying with all his might to keep J.D.'s arms pinned to the floor.

When he saw her he went very still. The laughter died

in his eyes, and they became very dark. He gently put Jed off his chest, shoved the dog out of his face and stood up. He studied her for so long she could feel her face begin to burn.

"Well, well, well," he finally said. "Isn't this a surprise?"

"I dress like this all the time," she lied.

"The grade five boys must be in heaven," he said.

"For Herbert," she exclaimed, and got just the reaction she wanted. He frowned. His eyebrows drew down over eyes that looked suddenly very black, and very menacing.

Jed spoiled it somewhat by clambering behind the couch and peeping out at her as if she was a perfect stranger.

And J.D. crossed the space between them, smiled ever so slightly and touched the tip of her ears.

A silly thing. A small thing. A thing that sent tingles up and down her spine.

"I don't believe you do dress like this for Herbert," he said softly, "which would mean you did it for me."

"I didn't!"

But he lowered his head, just as if she had said she did do it for him. Really, she should have seen it coming. And maybe she did see it coming. And maybe she wanted to taste him again, just because he was forbidden fruit.

He kissed her. It was as different from that kiss she had experienced on his front porch as night was from day, and it was different than that brief kiss in her motel room last night, too. His lips were soft, tender, questing. When they touched hers, her heart felt like a butterfly unfolding into flight within her chest.

She felt something give in her, a slight parting of her lips, an invitation.

He pulled away immediately, and of course she had to

act as if he had stolen that kiss, as if she had not been a party to it at all, as if she had not surrendered, invited.

There seemed to be only one way to make that point. When he broke contact, she smacked him across the face with her open hand. But not nearly as hard as she should have.

He touched his cheek, unhurt, and that knowing smile never left his face.

For a woman who prided herself on her control, she did seem to have a passionate reaction to him.

"I didn't put on this dress for you," she snapped. "Don't flatter yourself." But even she could feel the heat in the tips of her ears.

She spent an absolutely miserable evening at Herbert's nibbling dreadful cookies imported from England and sipping weak coffee. Herbert was gracious enough not to comment on her appearance, though as the evening progressed she wondered if he'd even noticed it in more than passing.

J.D. did not seem to be passing any kind of judgement on Herbert. In fact, the two men seemed to be getting on famously. They both loved cars. And football.

But if J.D. was not passing judgement on Herbert, why was she? Suddenly he seemed smaller, and infinitely more dull than he ever had before.

In his presence, J.D. seemed more vital, more handsome, more powerful, more charming, more everything.

And neither man seemed the least bit interested in her. Did either of them try to draw her into the conversation? No. Did either of them say the kind of flattering things a dress like this invited? No. Did either of them show one little bit of interest in her life? No.

She decided, childishly, that she hated them both.

She was never the childish one! She'd been so grown-

up, so adult, since she was about eight. Her family had
counted on her maturity in the face of Elana's illness.

After awhile, she got up and went into the kitchen.
Neither of them appeared to notice. She eyed the stainless
steel appliances, and went and ran her palm down the
front of the fridge. Sure enough, a big, ugly streak mark
was left.

From the kitchen she went into the hall. She was going
to slip out the door unnoticed and walk home, when she
spotted J.D.'s keys on the antique table at the entryway
where she had seen him leave them. She hesitated only
briefly, and then took them. By the time she started the
truck engine she was laughing out loud.

She wasn't really good with a standard and she supposed it was the grinding of the gears that brought J.D.
and Herbert to the window. With a jaunty wave, she abandoned him there.

Immature. Silly. Childish. Vindictive.

She really could not remember the last time she had
felt so darned happy.

"Gosh," Herbert said, watching the taillights disap-
pear. "Tally just wasn't herself tonight. That isn't like
her. To just leave without saying goodbye. She didn't say
goodbye, did she?"

"She not only didn't say goodbye," J.D. said, "she
swiped my truck."

"Oh, no, she would never do that. Tally isn't like that."

But Tally was being like that, because the truck was
disappearing from view.

"She's probably coming back," Herbert said. "She
probably noticed I was out of cream or something. She's
thoughtful."

It seemed to J.D. that Herbert was no kind of expert on

Tally, because J.D. knew Tally had not gone to get cream, was not being thoughtful and was not coming back.

He slid Herbert an assessing look. He really hadn't expected to like the guy quite so much. Nice guy, but obviously the absentminded professor type. The man had barely noticed the black dress, and J.D. had barely been able to breathe all night.

Every time she'd crossed her legs, sighed, shifted, he'd had to focus very hard to catch what Herbert was saying. His mind had been *glued* on her while he discussed vintage cars with Herbert.

An hour later Herbert finally figured out she wasn't coming back. "It's really not like her," he said, as if he had to apologize for her.

But J.D. had the happy suspicion that Tally Smith swiping his truck was probably more like her than anything she'd ever done before in her whole life. Why, there was a bonafide brat hiding out inside of Miss Priss.

"I better go, too," he said. "Is there a motel close by?"

Herbert gave him instructions, and he walked out into the night, weighing his thoughts. He liked Herbert. He was a genuinely nice guy. Okay, he might not be Mr. Excitement, but Tally could have done a lot worse for herself and for Jed.

Herbert would be infinitely stable. A reliable kind of guy who would provide a solid home for J.D.'s son. He was the kind of guy who would help with homework and give good financial advice and drive to hockey games early in the morning.

J.D. felt he should have been ecstatic that Tally had found such a good man to help her in the hard, hard job of raising a child.

But ecstasy was about the furthest thing from his mind. Because for all that Herbert was all right for Jed, he was all wrong for Tally. Geez, the guy had barely noticed the black dress. And he had no idea Tally needed to lose control. He had no idea that the woman who'd stolen a truck and left a man stranded might well be the real Tally.

J.D. hoped she had been laughing when she did it. At the thought of her delighting in her newfound devilment, his own smile curled up inside him, until he could restrain it no more. Walking down the quiet streets of Dogwood Hollow, J. D. Turner laughed out loud.

He'd caught a glimpse of the real Tally Smith, and it had nothing to do with that black dress.

He found the motel, and did a pretty good job of bluffing that he had a truck and luggage parked out in the darkness of their lot.

He went in and had a leisurely shower, lolled around in his underwear, watched TV until very late, celebrated the joys of being single.

There was really no excuse for him looking up her number and waiting until after midnight to call. He could tell by her voice she hadn't been sleeping, either.

"Just called to check on my dog," he said, "and my truck."

"Both are quite safe," she said coldly. "The horrible dog is right in bed with Jed. I would have never allowed it, but Kailey did."

Despite the coldness in her tone, he liked her voice reaching across to him in the night. "Dogs are meant to sleep with boys. It has to do with rule number three."

"Rule number three?"

"Nothing. How's my truck?"

"Totaled," she said. "I ran into a bus on the way home. Night blind. I told you."

"Do you have a sense of humor hiding under that no-nonsense veneer?"

"No," she said. "Good night, J.D."

He told himself not to say it. He told himself to hang up the phone. But there was his voice saying, "Tally, one more thing."

"Yes?"

"You looked pretty damn fine in that dress."

Silence. And then a dial tone. He could feel the smile deep inside him as he hung up the phone.

But if he had caught a glimpse of her last night, she had put it away by morning. When he showed up at the apartment, she was dressed in a white blouse with a cameo at the throat. She had on a purple sweater over top of it, and shapeless black pants. Her hair had been tortured back in such a tight bun her eyes were faintly slanted.

He thought it was just about the ugliest outfit and hairdo he had ever seen—designed to throw fear into the hearts of grade five children.

She was packed and ready to go. He noted that she had packed as if they were going to be spending three months on a camel crossing the Sahara.

"Did you bring five gallons of water in case the truck breaks down in the boonies?" he asked. "How about mittens? It's June, but you never know."

"You think I'm overdoing it, but you've never traveled with a small child, have you?"

Oh, boy. She was back to being her controlled self, in a big way. Really, he had to wonder if two weeks was going to be long enough to get her to break loose, to get her to let down her hair.

For Jed's sake, of course. Because if Herbert wasn't good for Tally, in the long run it wasn't going to be good for Jed either. J.D. knew from firsthand experience the impact an unhappy mother had on the whole family.

Sighing, he picked up the first round of suitcases. After

saying goodbye to Kailey, and getting the car seat adjusted, they were finally ready to go.

Jed's car seat had fit correctly in only one position in the truck, the passenger seat next to the window.

So now he found himself with Tally in the center position on the bench seat, wedged tightly against his shoulder, his thigh touching hers. She had to dodge the stick shift every time he put the truck into fourth gear or reverse. The dog was on the floor, whining piteously and trying to climb into the car seat with Jed.

After fifteen minutes, just as they had left Dogwood Hollow, and were settling in to the trip, Jed began flapping his arms and legs. "There yet?"

"Don't look so glum," J.D. said, deliberately putting a little more pressure on her thigh. "We're going to have some fun. Do you know what that is?"

She gave him a withering look and moved her leg as much as she was able. He chased it until they were touching again. "Of course I know what it is!"

"Give me some examples then."

"Sitting curled up on my couch with a good book. That's what I had planned for the first two weeks of summer holidays."

J.D. shot her a pitying look. "I knew that was the problem. Too much reading."

"Reading is a good thing," she said tersely. "All the experts agree that early reading skills are a precursor to lifelong success."

"Uh-huh. Let's read about people having fun instead of actually going out and doing it. And what the hell is a precursor? The word you say before you curse? In this case that would have been the *the* before the hell, am I correct little Miss Schoolteacher?"

She chose to ignore him, and rustled through a big bag of entertaining items she had brought for Jed.

J.D. didn't have any intention of being ignored. That was the advantage of being trapped in the truck with her. That, and the way her leg felt pressed against his. "And what's this lifelong success stuff? You're not planning Jed's whole life out for him, are you?"

"Of course not. I'm just providing learning opportunities."

"You're planning his whole life out for him," J.D. said darkly. "What have you decided. Doctor?"

"Are you insinuating there would be something wrong with your son becoming a doctor?"

"Terrible hours," J.D. said. "Inside work. Frankly, I don't think it's very manly."

"I'm sure I don't even want to know what you think manly is."

"Don't worry about that," he muttered. "You're going to find out."

She shot him a look, fished a storybook from that overflowing bag. She began reading it to Jed as if J.D. wasn't even there. But he noticed she wasn't trying very hard to escape the pressure of his leg.

It was a truly dull story about a little boy's day at the beach. The next one was about a pony.

J.D. rolled his eyes when she was finished. "See? Just like I said. Stories about someone else having fun. Wouldn't a real trip to the beach have been better? A real pony?"

"We are a long way from the nearest beach in case you haven't noticed!" she said.

"Pony?" Jed said hopefully.

"And your idea of having fun would be?" she said, arching her eyebrows at him.

Having you down on the ground on a blanket, and kiss-
ing you senseless. The black dress would be a nice touch.

"Being spontaneous," he said. "For instance, see that
dirt road over there? Don't you wonder where it goes?"

"No."

"For someone who reads a lot, you have a limited
imagination. Let's go see where it goes."

"No."

"May I remind you, you are not in charge?" And he
stomped on the brake and turned the wheel so fast his
truck skidded around in a half circle and they were bounc-
ing down a dirt road in the blink of an eye.

He felt her fingers dig into his arm. Her leg pressed
tighter to him.

"You are going too fast," she said.

He deliberately flexed his arm under her fingers. She
sighed almost inaudibly.

Jed screamed happily. "Go fast, J.D., faster."

The way he said J.D. made it sound suspiciously close
to Daddy.

J.D. obliged.

"Stop it," she bit out. "Stop it. We are going the
wrong way. At this rate we will never get to Dancer."

"So? If it takes us a couple of days to get there, big
deal. The object is for Jed and I to get to know one another."

"You are driving insanely! What if another car came
along this road?"

"This is the prairies. You can see another vehicle coming for twenty miles."

He soared over a little rise in the road, and the truck
took air. They landed so hard, her head fell against his
shoulder, and the first little hairs began to escape the bun.
Jed screamed with delight, and the dog howled.

"This holiday officially started the second we got out of that stuffy apartment," J.D. informed her.

"*Stuffy?* My apartment? I have placed myself in the care of a madman," she decided out loud.

The truck took air again. She screamed.

Jed and J.D. laughed. And then the breakthrough happened. She laughed, too. She actually laughed out loud as they raced down a deserted dirt road in the middle of nowhere, grabbing air and careening through puddles.

"That's better," J.D. said, glancing at her.

"I am not happy!" she said. "It's nerves."

As they came across the next rise, they surprised a herd of antelope. J.D. stopped the truck and they watched awe-struck as the amazingly graceful animals bounded away. Jed clapped and crowed.

J.D. watched Tally's face as she watched the beauty of the animals. She looked like she was going to cry.

"There's always a reward when you follow your heart," J.D. said.

"No, there isn't," she said. "There's always a heart-break when you follow your heart. Elana chased impulse after impulse and it led to her doom."

She was crying now, but she wiped impatiently at the tears.

"You need to learn that it's safe to let loose every now and then," he told her gently. "You need to learn that for Jed."

"You need to learn not to tell me what I need to learn," she said.

He threw back his head and laughed, and she actually saw the humor in it and smiled.

"Okay," she said. "I'm ready to try it."

"Letting loose?"

She nodded and held out her hand.

"What?"

"I'm driving."

"You're going to learn to let loose on my truck?" he asked with fake trepidation, handing her the keys, feeling secretly delighted that the woman in the black dress had been hiding very close to the surface.

"I'm afraid so."

Her eyes were shining, and bobby pins were sticking out of her hair at odd angles.

J.D. resisted the urge to reach over and help those bobby pins out of her hair. He had a feeling, if he wasn't careful at this stage, this could become the wildest ride of their lives. And it had absolutely nothing to do with driving a truck fast down a rutted road in the middle of the prairies.

"Get out," she ordered, "and take Jed with you."

"Huh?"

"I'm not endangering the lives of others while I let loose."

J.D. obliged her by going and setting his son free from the car seat. A moment later he and Jed and the dog stood in a cloud of dust as she took off. She hit the gas so hard the back of the truck slid sideways.

"Way to go, girl," he said.

A small hand crept into his. "Where auntie?"

"Oh, she's learning to let her devil out. Or swiping my truck. Either way, I'd say it's a great improvement over the impression of my maiden-aunt Matilda that she was doing earlier."

"Auntie Debil," Jed said approvingly.

"Oh," J.D. said, "with a little practice we could make your aunt really happy. Say it again. Auntie Devil. Good boy."

Chapter Six

Tally pulled away from them slowly. When J.D. and the dog and Jed were no more than three small specks on the prairie, she put her foot down a little harder on the gas pedal. The truck leapt forward, and she felt a little sensation of excitement and fear in her stomach. She went a little faster. The road was straight and uncomplicated. She went faster, still.

Then the truck rose over a little bump in the road, and crashed back down it.

She let out a little whoop, and slowed down long enough to unroll her window all the way. She could feel strands of hair being tugged out of the tight bun she had forced her hair into this morning as she picked up speed again.

She began to relax and then laughed at the sensation of power that coursed through her. "I embrace freedom," she yelled out her open window.

She felt instantly embarrassed and checked in her rearview mirror to see if anyone could have possibly heard her. When she realized they couldn't, she still felt embarrassed, but faintly elated at the very same time.

She felt so alive. The wind wafted a scent in her window of earth and sun and grass. In the distance, she could see the antelope herd, and a red-tailed hawk circled lazily above the prairie.

It must have been the fact that she was focused on the hawk, that made her miss the fact the road had changed, and was like a washboard underneath her tires. She could barely feel the ripples on the road in the cab of the truck, so when the bed began to sway dangerously it took her by surprise. She had no idea the horizontal ripples across the road would effect the performance of the truck! She tried to correct the sway with the steering wheel, but that only seemed to increase the snaking of the back end of the truck.

In desperation, she slammed on the brakes, and the truck heaved itself off the dirt road, spun one hundred and eighty degrees and stalled facing the way she had come.

Her heart was racing madly in her throat. She rested her head on the steering wheel and then shakily got out of the truck and leaned against the door, taking deep, steadying breaths.

"You," she told herself, "are not the adventurous type. A leopard cannot change its spots." Well, she was probably more like Bitsy-Mitsy than a leopard, but the idea was the same.

What she had needed, when she had taken those truck keys, was not to learn to drive fast. No, she had accepted J.D.'s challenge because she had needed a break from the pressure of J.D.'s leg against hers. That sensation had been overwhelming: the heated steel of his thigh muscle beneath faded denim, the masculine power that radiated from him, Tally becoming more and more aware of the

raw sensuality of the man. Nothing in her world had prepared her for the fact a man's leg touching hers like that
could make her feel…hungry.

A deep-down wild hunger like nothing she had ever
felt.

A hunger to tangle lips and touch skin and undo buttons
and run your fingers through hair the color of loam, that
promised to feel like silk. A renegade hunger to be
touched by strong male hands, touched on her cheeks and
earlobes, and her throat and her shoulders, and yes, in all
those places where she had never been touched.

It made her blush just to think about it. How on earth
was she going to get herself to Dancer without giving in
to the wild temptation J. D. Turner posed? Six hours she
might be able to manage, if she divided her time between
reading to Jed and keeping her nose in her own book. But
side trips? Unpredictable moments? *Embracing freedom?*

She looked at her watch. They had been embarked on
this journey for less than a full hour.

It was her second full day of being out of control. Okay,
she had survived, but her near incident with the truck had
been a chilling reminder that her survival, thus far, might
have been just luck.

In two days she had broken her building's rules, worn
a black dress that was completely unsuitable for the occasion and stolen a man's truck. She was an engaged
woman who had kissed a man who was not her fiancé
three times. And now she was feeling complicated little
stirrings in her stomach from the mere touch of his leg.

If she was smart, she would head that truck back around
and follow that red-tailed hawk to who knew where. But
that was no more in her nature than black dresses, stealing
trucks, fantasizing more kisses. And what about Jed? She
had to go back for Jed.

"You have no choice," she told herself, firmly and contemplated her dislike of those words.

Of course she had a choice! Perhaps not over the circumstances but over the way she reacted to them!

It had been childish and silly for her to let loose on the prairie with a truck. She was not a truck driver. She was not a speed demon! She was not an adventurer, or a daredevil.

From now on, she would be herself! Her reactions would be under control, if nothing else in her whole life was. With this new resolve, Tally climbed back in the truck and used the rearview mirror to fix her hair, sticking the pins in so viciously it hurt her own scalp.

But as she headed back, despite the set of her shoulders, and her steely resolve, she felt as if she was driving straight toward the thing she was most afraid of.

And suddenly she knew that wasn't J. D. Turner.

It was that hunger burning deep in her belly—the secrets within herself—that she was most afraid of losing control over.

She drove back extra slowly, and finally saw J.D. and Jed in the distance. It was obvious they were having an absolute blast together. As she got closer she could see that Beauford had something between his teeth, and the boy and man were chasing after him trying to retrieve whatever it was.

It was a joyous sight. The boy and man chasing the dog, the sun bright around them, last year's grass mingled with new growth so high around them that sometimes the dog disappeared. It was a sight that made Tally yearn to lose control all over again.

She got closer, and pulled over. She might actually have let herself feel some vicarious pleasure from this happy scene had it not been for the fact the dog veered close to the truck and she got a very good view of what he had clenched so happily in his big, slobbery mouth.

The storybook about the beach!

Here she had given J.D.'s idea of fun a fair chance—and almost been killed doing it—and he was showing nothing but contempt for her values and ideas!

"Hi," J.D. called to her as she got out of the truck, just as if his dog was not mocking her, "how was your wild adventure?"

"I was almost killed," she said. "I nearly had an accident."

He was at her side in one long stride, and she found her shoulders locked in his powerful grasp, his eyes scanning her face. "Are you hurt?"

There was that tingle again. That awareness so strong it stung. He hadn't even glanced at his truck.

A woman embracing freedom, learning to love her adventurous side, might read something into that, but one committed to maintaining control could not afford to give up anymore of herself to his easy charm.

"No, I'm not hurt." She didn't add, *no thanks to you,* but he seemed to hear it anyway.

The audacity of the man. His facial expression changed from one of compelling concern to one of insulting skepticism. "What kind of accident could you have out here?" he asked, gesturing to the broad expanse of nearly flat land.

"I went over some washboard. I lost control of the back end of the truck and spun around."

He regarded her thoughtfully, and waited. When she added nothing else, he prodded, "Are you getting to the nearly killed part soon?"

"That is the nearly killed part," she informed him.

"Scared you, huh?" He was looking at her much too

closely, seeing things she did not want him—or anyone—
to see. Her vulnerability. She had the awful feeling he
was going to put his arms around her. The thing she most
needed to avoid if she was going to keep this hard-won
control was any kind of physical contact with him.

"It did not scare me!" she said, backing away from
him. "It made me realize how absurd it was for me to be
racing along some rutted road as if I was queen of the
four-wheel drive crowd. What if the truck had flipped
over? What if Jed had been in it?"

He chucked her on the chin. "*What if* is a bad question
for the overly imaginative," he said calmly.

"You're dismissing my very real concerns as imagination? And allowing your dog to destroy my property at
the same time?"

"You came back with your armor on. Every hair in
place, too, I see. You really did put a scare into yourself.
But I wonder if it was about the truck doing a little spin."

To be read so easily was humiliating! "It was not little," she said through clenched teeth. "And I want my
book back from that dog. That is no way to teach a
child—or a dog—to treat books."

"We've been trying to get it back," he said, not sound-
ing properly contrite at all. "But old Beau has never had
so much fun."

"Well as long as Beau is having fun," she said sarcas-
tically and gave him the Ms. Smith-is-displeased-look that
worked so well on children. He grinned at her unfazed!

She stepped sideways around him. "Beauford, come
here."

The dog hesitated in his romping, gazed between her
and Jed and back again, undecided.

"This instant!" she said.

Giving Jed a regretful look, the dog slunk over to her,

his head down, his tail tucked tight between his legs, the book clenched between his teeth.

"That's a good dog," she crooned, but when she lunged for the book, Beauford took a crafty step sideways. She took a faster step toward him, grabbed and missed again.

She could see the merriment shining in that dog's beady brown eyes. Well, she was not having a dog get the best of her. She lunged. The dog moved. And the next thing she knew she was chasing it, screaming.

Out-of-control again, she realized, and brought herself up short while she still had a tiny bit of her dignity left untattered. She deliberately turned her back on the dog.

"Jed, it's time for us to go." In an undertone to J.D. she said, "You get my book back right now."

"Oh, yes ma'am," he said, snapping her an insulting salute.

She took Jed's hand firmly and ignoring his protests, strapped him back into his seat in the truck.

Out of the corner of her eye, she saw J.D. walk right up to the stupid beast, give him a command with his hand to sit. Another hand command and the book was dropped neatly on the ground. J.D. stooped, picked it up and came over to her, handing it to her.

She held it at the corner eyeing the dog saliva.

J.D. took it back and wiped it on his shirt, then handed it back to her. "He's soft with his mouth," he said, "like a bird dog. He didn't hurt it. There isn't even a tooth mark on it."

"It is still an unforgivable way to treat a book. That's not the type of lesson I want Jed learning."

"That's okay," J.D. said, but she could see the tightness around his own mouth. "I have many other things to teach him."

"Wite name," Jed informed her.

"You wrote your name?" she asked, confused and pleased, nonetheless. All those hours on the floor with the alphabet blocks finally paying off. It was a disappointment that it had happened with J.D., instead of with her, but still he was four. It was an accomplishment to be proud of, nothing at all like tearing down a dirt road in a truck.

It occurred to her she had not packed the alphabet blocks.

"With pee-pee," Jed chortled.

"That's one of the many other things you have to teach him?" she inquired of J.D. through lips so tight they hardly moved.

"Handy once it snows," J.D. said without an ounce of contrition. "How about if you handle the book stuff, and I handle the boy stuff?"

"Well, I never," she said.

"Lady, that is written all over you in sky-high letters."

"What do you mean?"

"You know darn well what I mean."

"I don't."

"Okay let me spell it out to you. It's obvious that you have never. And it's obvious why."

He was stepping way over the line! Unless she was mistaken, and she knew she was not, he was referring to her most intimate secrets—or lack thereof.

How could he know she hadn't ever? That wasn't possible! Unless he had felt her hunger when her leg was pressed against his in the too-small cab of that truck. She tried to think back. Had she trembled with desire? Given herself away in some way? What a mortifying thought!

"How would you know what I have never done?" she said, her voice like ice, but her heart beating wildly in her chest.

"I could taste it on your lips," he said.

"You are being far too familiar!" she said.

"Oh, well."

She should have left it at that, really. "And what is your theory about why I have never?" she said, injecting as much scorn into her voice as she could.

"Because you are an uptight prig that no man in his right mind would ever try to get close to. Gee, getting close to you would be like snuggling up to a porcupine. Prickle, prickle, prickle."

"You are wrong," she said, "Dead wrong." Though of course he wasn't. It felt like the prickle, prickle, prickle was happening behind her eyes!

"Yeah, well," he said, "prove it."

She stared at him. Oh, how she would have loved to throw herself at him, take those smug lips with her own, curl her tongue around his, make him beg her to do that thing she had never done with him.

"Ooh," he said cruelly, "the little lady is thinking of playing with fire. Remember what your momma told you. Or was it your grade five teacher? You'll get burned."

It was infuriating that he was right. She had too little experience to think she was going to get the upper hand with him by kissing him. She would just end up with a life more out of control than ever.

Burned, as he had so kindly put it.

"I think we need to get to Dancer as soon as possible."

"No kidding," he muttered, "you probably need to sharpen your quills."

Always the tease, always making light at her expense.

"So I can get a motel and slam the door in your face," she said.

"Happy to be able to give you a thrill," he said amiably.

They drove back to the highway in simmering silence. *"J-e-d,"* Jed sang happily, oblivious to the mood in the cab of the truck, "wite it in pee."

J.D. snuck a little look at the woman sitting beside him. Her spine was straight and stiff. She was pushed over against that child's car seat as far as she could get. Somehow, her leg was not touching his, though the space between them was about the thickness of a sheet of paper, close enough that he could still feel the soft heat radiating from her.

She was going through that beach book with a fine-tooth comb looking for some hint of damage by Beauford. So she could sue him.

He sighed. He knew exactly what had gone wrong. Exactly. He'd given her too much too soon.

When she'd actually laughed about going fast he had mistakenly thought she was ready for bigger and better things.

It was like giving a glass of champagne to a ten-year-old. A sip or two they could handle. More than that, they couldn't.

She was mad as a wet hen. And not that she'd nearly had an accident either. That he had actually talked her into having fun. That's what she was mad about. Of course, after Elana, fun and disaster were probably linked fairly closely in her mind.

Something he was going to have to keep in mind next time.

And next time could not be too soon. If she managed to cement herself into this sour position, he might not be able to break through her armor again.

Still, opportunity did not present itself. She read to Jed

out of storybooks, and studiously ignored every one of J.D.'s efforts to make her laugh, or even speak.

They stopped, once, for hamburgers.

Jed tried to practice his new name-writing skill in the parking lot of the restaurant, which earned J.D. the silent treatment all through lunch and the rest of the way to Dancer.

Honestly, he should have been so glad to check her into the Palmtree, to be rid of her for the day. But instead he was aware of the ticking of the clock, the amount of time he had to complete this mission.

He went home and laid awake plotting new ways to make her cut loose, and laugh.

And thinking about the tinge that had changed the color of her cheeks when he had suggested she never had.

And wrestling with the question whether he owed it to his son to save Tally Smith from a passionless marriage.

Of course, the only way he could think of to do that, would be to introduce her to passion himself.

With anyone else it might have been an interesting exercise. But, oh, Ms. Smith was more complicated than the average woman.

And he suspected, under that bristly exterior, far more easily hurt. Sensitive.

You couldn't seduce a woman like her and walk away from it with a clean conscience, no matter how noble your motives. Of that, he was fairly certain.

Exhausted and confused, a soldier no longer so certain about the perimeters of his mission, he finally got up and made coffee.

It occurred to him he needed to define his mission, so he went to the kitchen, turned on the radio and got a pad of paper. He sat at the kitchen table and scowled at the blank piece of paper for a long time before he wrote across the top: What A Woman Should Know.

He thought again, hard, before he finally wrote.

One, a woman should know better than to settle in life for stainless steel appliances instead of wild nights of endless passion.

J.D. eyed what he had written and decided he wasn't quite ready to tackle number one yet.

Two, he wrote, a woman should know that too many rules were damaging to a small boy's spirit. Actually, to anyone's spirit. He put a small check mark beside that one because he could not help but feel, a trifle proudly, he was making a bit of headway in the rules department.

Three, he wrote, germs are rarely deadly. Dog kisses are one of life's delights. He actually knew the perfect place to take someone with a germ phobia, and he wrote mud bog in brackets behind number three.

Four could be tackled at the same time as three because it dealt with the fact that small boys—and big ones—*need* to get dirty.

Five, life needs to hold surprises.

He reread his list, and thought that was quite enough for any man to try and accomplish in two weeks.

And yet he could not still the pen. Almost of its own volition, it moved across the page and wrote: Six, Women who get married for security end up like dried old prunes, who don't laugh enough and are prone to depression in their middle years.

Well, a woman did need to know that! He could not shirk his duty by not confronting her with the fact that if she married a man who did not recognize the significance of a black dress there was no telling what kind of woman she would become.

It sickened J.D. thinking about it, though only, he told

himself, because of the eventual effect it would have on Jed.

Yes, he, J. D. Turner, had the obligation to stop it right now. Six little things that he had to teach her, two weeks to do it in.

There wasn't much time. He should start right now. He looked at his clock. Midnight.

There was not a thing he could do at this time of night. And then the radio announcer said, "And just a reminder that here in North Dakota we will have an amazing view of the meteor shower, predicted for 1:00 a.m."

A meteor shower! Divine intervention! She might not think stargazing at one in the morning was appropriate, but it was her rules that needed to be broken. It said so right here on his list. In fact, it was number two.

Whistling, J.D. put on water and made a carafe of hot chocolate. He grabbed his jacket and headed for the door.

A few minutes later he was at the Palmtree, knocking on her door. She opened it and regarded him warily.

He noticed she was wearing the same getup as before—high-collared, long-sleeved nightdress. But her hair was free, and it was beautiful, long and flowing. It made him want to run his fingers through it, to beg her to wear it like this all the time.

"What?" she asked. "What is it about you and nocturnal visits? Have you had another revelation?"

He sure had—that he had a lot of work to do on her, and not enough time to do it. He noticed she did not look like she had been sleeping, any more than he had. Perhaps a little more shaken up than she wanted to let on.

"Hi," he said cheerfully.

She glowered at him.

"I just heard on the radio there's going to be a meteor shower shortly. I didn't think Jed should miss it."

"Jed is four years old," she sputtered. "He is in bed sleeping at this outrageous hour, not up gallivanting."

"Gallivanting? Are you serious?" He could see she was, and though he would have loved to have given her some lessons in gallivanting, that would probably have to wait for another night. "I thought we could just wrap him up in a blanket. I'll hold him on my lap. Some things are too good to sleep through. Do you remember that movie where the kid sees the Russian rocket go over his house, and it changes his life forever?"

"So, tonight is going to change Jed's life forever?" Her words were skeptical, but he saw the softening in her eyes. He guessed she'd liked that movie. Probably showed it to all her grade fivers to get them excited about the science fair.

"It could," he said, thinking *if I can change you, I can change his life forever.*

"I don't know."

"I brought hot chocolate," he said, when he saw her wavering.

"I guess just once wouldn't hurt. Like Christmas Eve."

"Exactly," he said, careful not to push his advantage too hard. "I'll arrange the chairs, if you want to pour the hot chocolate."

He turned from her before she could rethink it. He'd learned something important. Her defenses were down slightly in the middle of the night.

The Palmtree had plastic lawn furniture in front of each cabin, and he found two chairs and positioned them in the middle of the parking lot.

He went and tapped lightly on the door and went in. She had a little kitchen unit this time, and she was at the counter watering down Jed's hot chocolate with milk. She had pulled a bulky sweater over her nightdress, and on anyone else it would have looked like a nightmare.

But on her somehow it didn't.

"You take Jed," she whispered, "and I'll take the co-coa."

He went and looked down into his son's sleeping face. A feeling so strong it could have knocked him off his feet came over him. A feeling of love, of wanting to protect, of wanting to change the whole world so that it would never give this little one heartache, or hurt.

She came and stood beside him. "He's beautiful, isn't he?" she said with such soft reverence.

He glanced at her, and was amazed to feel the very same feeling in his chest when he looked at her as he had felt when he looked at his son: a sensation of wanting to protect, of wanting to change the whole world to prevent her heartaches and hurts.

The feeling stunned him.

She was prickly! Porcupinelike! Controlling! Totally lacking a sense of humor.

But looking at her in the soft light of the motel room, gazing at her nephew, J.D. glimpsed her truth just as surely as he had glimpsed it when she wore a black dress, and when she stole his truck, and when she laughed out loud.

Prickly was her pretense, and her defense. What she really was, was something else entirely.

And for the first time since he had committed to this mission he wasn't at all sure that once he unleashed the real Tally Smith he was going to be able to handle it, control what happened next.

Because even now he wanted to do something stupid, lean toward her, touch the tip of her nose with his lips, tell her everything in her world would be okay.

Instead, he tucked the blankets close around Jed and scooped him up in his arms. The boy was painfully light. How could something so light, a weight so insignificant, change a man's whole world, change the way he thought and felt about everything?

Even his own future.

The boy stirred against him, and he tucked him tight to his chest, and strode outside. He got settled in a chair, the child in the crook of one arm, the hot chocolate in the other. She came and sat beside him, and gazed upward.

"Oh," she said, "it is so utterly beautiful."

And it was, even though the main event had not even started. That moment, sitting in the Palmtree parking lot in a plastic chair with a child on his lap and a beautiful woman beside him, and the stars winking gloriously in a black velvet night sky felt like it put every other beautiful moment of his whole life to shame.

Even the ones he had spent with Elana, singing her a love song.

Jed stirred against him, and his eyes fluttered open. "J.D.," he said, and his voice held a welcoming joy that made J.D. wonder how he had survived thus far in his lonely life.

"Hey, little buddy, we're going to look at some stars."

"Doggie here?"

"No. I left him at home."

Jed turned his face toward the sky, put his thumb in his mouth and contemplated it. "Vewy pwettee," he said around his thumb. He snuggled deep into J.D.'s chest.

From somewhere deep inside him, the song came. Softly, J.D. sang a love song to his son. "Annabel was a cow of unusual bovine beauty," he crooned.

His son smiled at him, settled deeper into his chest, and he sang on.

"Happy," Jed said when J.D. had finished the song. Tally was smiling.

"There's going to be a meteor shower," Tally said, when the silence of the night had enveloped them. She launched into a scientific explanation.

This obviously went right over Jed's head, but J.D. felt himself tingle oddly. What she was really saying, it seemed, was that now and then people got to be in the presence of miracles.

And that's how it felt to him, sitting in this parking lot, with his son on his lap, and that beautiful enigmatic woman beside him.

As if somehow, though he was completely unworthy of it, life had decided to give him a miracle.

What if his mission was not to change her, after all?

What if it was to change the thing in himself that had kept him from having moments like this all his life? That had kept him from saying yes to the greatest miracle of all?

It was the soft silkiness of the night air, the lateness of the hour, too many nights with not enough sleep that was filling his head with such foolishness.

"Do you know any of the constellations?" she asked.

"Oh, sure," he said, relieved to talk about something concrete, scientific. "The easy ones. The Big Dipper. The Little Dipper. Orion."

"I wish we had a telescope," she said dreamily. She took a sip of her hot chocolate and he noticed it left a little moustache. She tickled it off with her tongue, and he felt a burst of heat go through him that would put something like a meteor shower to shame.

They took turns finding constellations and trying to point them out to Jed, but he did not appear interested in giving things names. He seemed so attuned to the magic in the air.

And then the meteor shower began.

Jed's eyes went very wide. He cooed reverently as the scattered pieces of light danced and fell and raced through the brilliant sky. In a world of special effects and fireworks it should have seemed like a small thing, but somehow it didn't.

When it was over, they sat very still.

J.D. felt Jed relax against him, and then his breathing formed little warm clouds against J.D.'s chest.

"He's sleeping," he said.

"I think he'll never forget this, ever," she said, "Thank you."

Somehow J.D. had the feeling he was not going to forget this, ever, either, and that was not part of his plan.

He could make that all worse right now, if he leaned toward her, if he took advantage of the sudden tenderness in her eyes, the slackening of her guard.

But the idea had never been to change his life forever. He liked his life just fine, thank you. The idea had been to change her life.

And he knew if he stayed here one more minute nothing was going to go according to his plan.

So he stood up, shoved the sleeping child into her arms, ignored the astounded expression on her face, and said, "Well, that was fun. See you tomorrow. Sleep in."

Chapter Seven

Well, that was fun. See you tomorrow. Sleep in.

Tally stared at J.D.'s truck leaving the parking lot and snapped her mouth, which had fallen open, shut.

Of all the aggravating men! The night had been so magical. So wondrous. There had been a wonderful tingle in the air that had very little to do with the bits of meteor showering down around them.

And he left just like that?

A light blinked on in the motel office, and then the outside lights came on and bathed the parking lot, chasing away every last remnant of magic.

She felt very eccentric, indeed, sitting alone in the middle of a parking lot in the middle of the night with a sleeping child on her lap. Tally Smith, eccentric! The girl who had worked so hard to appear so normal her whole life.

Still, there was something just a tiny bit fun about someone entertaining the notion she might be eccentric.

If it didn't make it feel like J.D. was *winning* in some way, she might have enjoyed a little laugh about it.

"Everything okay, Ms. Smith?"

Just fine. Great. Never been better. Out loud she said, "Just watching the meteor shower."

"Oh." Pause. "I don't see nothin'."

That oh and the pause that followed it were loaded with lots of unspoken thoughts about eccentric people.

"It's over," she said patiently.

She swaddled the blankets around Jed, and lugged him back into the cabin. She tucked him into his bed, brushed the hair back from his eyes, and smiled, feeling that familiar tug of love for him.

He opened his eyes, blinked at her, closed them again. "Wonderful," he said happily. "So pwettee."

She sighed, leaned over and kissed the round fullness of his cheek. "Yes," she said, "it was that."

She tugged off her own sweater and crawled into the other bed. "Sleep," she ordered herself. She could not remember a time in her life when she had kept such irregular hours. She should be exhausted.

Instead she thought exhaustively about him, J. D. Turner, his face turned up to the stars, his strong arms folded around the little boy she cherished, the low, beautiful rasp of his voice as he sang that song. She thought of the shape of his lips, how the planes of his face looked gilded in moonlight.

Tally sat straight up in bed. "You are engaged to another man," she told herself sternly. "What are you thinking of J. D. Turner for?"

He was not her fiancé. He was not the man she was going to marry!

She knew drastic measures were called for. She needed to do a reality check. Dogwood Hollow was her reality.

Teaching grade five and staying on the main roads was her reality. Herbert Henley, and his hardware store, and his stainless steel appliances were her reality.

Herbert was probably not going to appreciate what an important moment this was in their relationship, a pivotal moment, but she was choosing him as her reality touchstone, and she had never needed one more.

Resolutely she picked up the phone beside her bed and dialed Herbert's number. She tried very hard not to look at the red digital numbers on the clock. She was pretty sure Herbert was not going to be able to remember the last time he was up at two in the morning, either.

She was about to hang up after the eighth ring, when his sleepy voice answered the phone.

"Hi, Herbert, it's Tally."

"Tally?" She could hear him groping around, knew the precise moment he found his glasses and looked at the clock. "Is something wrong?"

"No, I just wanted to hear your voice."

The silence was long and surprised. "Oh. When the phone rang I thought there must be something wrong at the hardware store."

"No...I just missed you." The words tasted like dust in her mouth.

"Oh...my."

Well, what was she expecting at two in the morning? The truth was that she was expecting, *I really miss you, too, Tally.*

After a long silence, he ventured, "How was the drive?"

He had to ask that! What was she going to answer? *I had a wild moment of freedom and I'm terrified I could become addicted to moments like that?*

"The drive was fine," she said, and then wondered if

their conversations were always so wooden, so lacking in enthusiasm.

Of course they weren't! She'd called at two in the morning. She felt like the whole life she had planned for herself was dissolving in front of her and desperate, she said, "I was thinking, Herbert, we should probably set a date."

"A date," he said, baffled. "For what?"

"Our wedding!" She could hear a faintly hysterical note in her voice.

"Oh, that. There's no rush is there?"

But suddenly it did feel to her like there was a rush. A terrible rush. Because if she didn't commit to him, totally and irrevocably, she had the uneasy feeling that alarming and unpredictable things were going to happen.

"I just thought maybe we should solidify things between us." It occurred to her, her wording was not in the least romantic.

"Could we discuss this some other time?" His voice sounded plaintive. Did she hear a little edge of panic in it? As if maybe he didn't want to set a date? Of course not. She had called him in the middle of the night. He was half-asleep and surprised. This was really a totally unfair thing for her to do to him.

"How about in general terms?" she said. "As in were you thinking, fall?"

"This fall?" he squeaked.

"Or winter, or spring?"

"This isn't like you," he said.

"I know," she said sadly.

"How about we talk about it when you get home?"

"Sure, that would be fine."

"Bye, love," and he hung up the phone with unseeming swiftness.

Bye, love was not the same as *I love you*. Had she ever told Herbert she loved him? She didn't think so. It wasn't that kind of relationship. It wasn't about flowers and stolen kisses and midnight phone calls.

She realized she had not said the words *I love you* to Herbert, because she did not love him. She liked him. She respected him.

"You're using him," she said out loud and felt a terrible wave of shame. But why should she feel ashamed? He knew it was not a grand passion.

But did he know she wanted a stable home for her nephew, the boy she had been charged with raising? Did Herbert know he had been chosen, not because he stirred her heart, but because he was the safest of men? The man least likely to do a crazy thing, or to make her do a crazy thing?

Didn't that fear live inside her? That she was Elana's sister. That somewhere in her resided a well of craziness that could blow her world apart?

She could feel the craziness stirring in her now. And with it a deep resentment for J. D. Turner, who had really turned her life inside out without half-trying.

Viewing meteor showers in the middle of the night. Racing down dirt roads. Kissing strangers on his front step.

Oh, she wished she would not have thought of his lips. They were the very thing that could bring out the crazy in her.

And it did.

Because she found herself reaching for the phone again, dialing another number.

"Hello?"

She didn't say anything for a second, just let the sound of his deep voice caress her spine like a shiver.

"Hi, Tally," he said, his voice rough with sleep, but not irritated.

"How did you know it was me?" Had she really been going to hang up without identifying herself, before he had guessed it was her? She was not a prank caller!

"Just a guess." His voice was low and teasing, amused. Sexy. There was no getting around that. His voice was sexy.

"I'm not the type of woman who makes middle-of-the-night phone calls."

"You know what?" he said softly. "I don't think either of us knows what kind of woman you are."

"I do!" she protested, though who she was seemed to be wavering in her own mind like an oasis in a desert mirage.

He chuckled. "I'm glad you phoned. Life needs some surprises."

Well, her life was certainly turning out to be surprising. The man who was supposed to enjoy hearing from her in the middle of the night, hadn't been the least bit pleased by the sound of her voice! And J.D. sounded, well, distinctly happy that it was her.

"So, what's up?" She heard rustling, pictured him sitting up in bed, plumping the pillow behind his head, settling in to talk to her, not trying to figure out how to get rid of her. He'd be like a cat, relaxed and alert at the very same time.

It occurred to her she had not pictured what Herbert looked like in bed.

She forced herself to contemplate that now. She pictured Herbert, in flannel, button-up pajamas with a monogram over the pocket.

And she bet J.D. wore nothing at all.

"Well, goodbye," she said, hastily, thankful for the

anonymity of the phone. J.D. couldn't tell what she was thinking, couldn't feel the heat in her cheeks.

"Hey, wait a sec. Did you phone for a reason?"

If she hadn't phoned for a reason, what would he think?

"I called to tell you Herbert and I are setting a date," she said in a rush.

Silence. And then his voice, deep, calm, sensuous as a touch, "I think I probably could have waited until morning to hear that."

What did that mean? That he didn't want her to set a date? That he didn't want her to marry someone else? She could not let her mind go there. All her carefully laid plans for the future would be threatened if she let her mind go there.

"Actually, I didn't call to say that," she said, clearly babbling like an idiot, and just as clearly unable to stop herself, "I called to thank you, for the meteor shower. I know it's something that Jed will remember for the rest of his life."

"Great. I'm glad."

"Okay. Good night."

"Good night, sweetheart."

"Oh! I have asked you not to call me that."

He laughed, a deep low rumble that made her tingle all over. "Sorry. I forgot the rules. Perfectly understandable in the middle of the night, wouldn't you say?"

"I suppose."

"Have you ever considered the possibility you have too many rules?"

"Never."

"How's a man supposed to remember them all?"

This was all wrong. Herbert couldn't wait to get rid of her, and she couldn't get J.D. to hang up the phone.

J.D. who called her sweetheart, and was teasing her.

It didn't mean anything. She knew that. If his dog was a female, he'd call her sweetheart. He'd called the waitress that at the hamburger joint where they had stopped for lunch. The waitress, young and chubby and not at all attractive, had looked like he'd given her the greatest tip of her day.

So, it was just his way. Still, there was something rather delightful about lying burrowed down deep in your covers, the phone cradled against your ear, and a man's deep voice on the other end, calling you sweetheart.

"I have to go," she said.

"Hmmm. Well, thanks for calling. What date did you set?"

"I said we are setting a date, not that we have."

"I see the distinction."

"I wish you wouldn't make fun of me."

"You're the one who called. It's kind of like asking for it."

She considered this for a moment. She had always thought girls who phoned boys were the kind who were asking for it.

Is that what he thought? Was there a double meaning to what he had just said?

"Well, goodbye. See you tomorrow." *Hang up the phone,* she ordered herself, but she didn't. Neither did he.

When the silence had stretched long enough, she said, "What did you have planned for tomorrow? Just so I'll know what to wear."

"I have something dirty planned."

His voice seemed like a low, sensuous growl. She gasped. See, she had phoned him in the middle of the night, and he had assumed she was the kind of girl that asked for it, and now he was planning something dirty.

"Dress appropriately," he said, and hung up the phone.

She stared at the receiver for a long time before she managed to put the receiver back on the cradle.

Something dirty. Dress appropriately. Good grief, she had a child with her. What was he thinking?

She shivered and tried to work herself into a proper state of indignation about it, but the truth was she felt warm and delicious as she thought dreadfully naughty thoughts, snuggled under her covers and slept.

J.D. hung up the phone, folded his arms behind his head and stared at the ceiling. Tally Smith had phoned him. In the middle of the night.

And he was willing to bet there was nothing about that in Tally Smith's long and convoluted rule book.

Which meant he could put a little check mark beside item number two on his list. She was learning rules were meant to be broken. There was hope for her after all.

And she had allowed herself to be surprised tonight. So that was two things with check marks beside them on his list.

But he could see something he hadn't quite expected. He couldn't just cross those things off the list, as if they'd been accomplished. It would take repetition and practice to truly convert her to a more relaxed way of thinking.

He thought of the meteor shower, the child in his arms, Tally next to him, the song that had bubbled out of him. He thought of glancing over at her and seeing her face tilted toward the stars, her expression so earnest and full of wonder.

Who had really been surprised? Him or her?

He'd been the one who blinked first, who had left on the run. He'd left the Palmtree parking lot like a scared pup. Tally relaxed and happy was quite a bit more dangerous a proposition than Tally uptight and rule-bound.

He wondered, not for the first time, if he was playing a game of which he couldn't control the outcome.

But no, she had phoned.

Amazing progress, really. Now was no time to doubt himself. To give up. Especially since she had sounded a little bit intrigued about getting dirty. Who would have guessed?

He thought he could probably combine lessons three and four; that germs are rarely deadly and that small boys and big ones need to get dirty.

And then it would be a week or two of reinforcement of all the lessons she had learned, and he could send her home, confident in the knowledge that she knew what a woman should know.

But send her home to what?

A man who would take that newfound thing within her and kill it deader than a doornail? J.D. had to contemplate that for a minute.

Tally Smith and Herbert Henley were setting a date? A wedding date?

He hated that. And he didn't even want to think why he hated it, why there was a burning in his chest, and a restlessness in his soul that made him want to throw something, or break something, or rip something apart.

As if he wasn't working himself into enough of a lather, another thought chased through his mind.

Of Tally with Herbert. Intimate.

He considered getting up, storming through the house and throwing his engine right off the kitchen counter and out the window—without opening the window first.

"Hold it there, pal," he said. He studied his ceiling suspiciously, trying to figure out exactly what she had been trying to tell him.

The problem with a woman was that they spoke in

codes nearly unbreakable by a man of average intelligence. He looked at the clock, hesitated and then picked up the phone. He dialed information first, and then dialed the number.

"Hi? Is this Herbert? J. D. Turner, here. No, no, Tally's fine. I just wondered if you could answer a question for me. Well, I know three in the morning is a slightly unusual time to call, but I'm new to this daddy stuff and I tend to keep myself awake worrying about it. So this was my question—when you and Tally get hitched, what kind of notice do I need to give Jed? I mean all of us would have to decide exactly what to tell him of course, but—

"You and Tally are not getting married in the foreseeable future? You're telling me I don't have to say anything to him right now? Good, good. That's all I really wanted to know. Thanks, Herbert. You seem like a real good guy." He almost said he thought he would make a terrific dad for his son, but somehow the words just got caught in his throat.

He hung up the phone, and thought, his worries assuaged, that he could go right to sleep now.

But instead he wondered about a man who wouldn't show a little more curiosity about another man calling wanting information about his wedding.

Didn't Herbert feel slightly possessive of Tally? Protective? Didn't he feel jealous? Now that J.D. thought about it, it seemed strange that Herbert was okay with Tally getting in a truck with a strange man and driving halfway across the country with him.

It seemed very plain to him that Herbert didn't love Tally.

He found that hard to believe. She was so beautiful and smart and tender. Prickly, but that was just a cover for all that softness underneath.

It was very plain to him that in order for Tally to fully understand number one and six on his list, she was going to have to give up Herbert.

He glanced at his clock and groaned. Ever since the moment he had heard knocking on his door interrupting his rendition of ''Annabel the Cow'' his life had been on a collision course. With what he hadn't been certain, until now.

Now he was fairly certain he was on a collision course with destiny.

''Just introduce her to the greatest mud bog in the world, and don't complicate your life,'' J.D. ordered himself. He wondered, grimly, if he was ever going to sleep again.

Of course, she had a talent for complicating things.

The next morning he showed up at the motel with a lunch packed by the diner. As usual Tally hadn't followed directions.

He'd said to be prepared to get dirty, and he was dressed for the mud bog. His oldest shirt, his jeans with the knee out and the rear worn just about through.

And here she was, all dressed in white!

And not in virginal white, either. No sirree, Tally Smith was dressed in a way he had never quite seen before, and he had trouble keeping his eyes inside his head.

Tally Smith was wearing a white shirt, open over what looked to be a lacy little camisole. The slacks were form-fitting.

And did the lady ever have a form.

Her hair was loose and she'd done something with her eyes. Makeup. It made her eyes look huge and sultry.

Herbert was insane. That was all there was to it. Could he really let the guardian of his child marry an insane man?

Jed flew into his arms, thankfully dressed in overalls. J.D. picked his son up and swung him around until every bit of confusion in his heart had melted into that little boy's laughter.

"So," he said as he put the truck in gear, "you ready for some mud bogging?"

"Some what?"

"Four-wheel driving in mud. It's fun. I told you to be prepared to get dirty."

She looked at him with horror, and then her face turned bright, bright red.

He felt himself draw in the air so sharply he whistled. "Did you think I meant, um, something else?"

"Don't be absurd," she said tightly.

But he snuck another glance at the outfit. Tally Smith had thought he meant a different kind of dirty. And she'd dressed for it! So she knew Herbert was a mistake. She knew it!

But she was getting ready to throw her wild side at him? At J. D. Turner?

And where had she got the idea that *dirty* expressed all the wonderful things that happened between a man and a woman?

His list of things she needed to know seemed to be expanding rather than getting smaller! There was a strangled silence in the cab of the truck, broken only by the happy sighs of the dog as Jed bent over double in his car seat trying to kiss him.

They took a secondary road out of Dancer, and then turned onto an unmarked trail over the prairie. The road dipped and twisted over rolls in the land, and then dipped one final time into a natural depression in the earth. A sea of muck, the size of a football field, awaited.

"This is the mud bog," J.D. said, his voice like a tour

guide who was thinking of things far more interesting than what he was pointing out to the tourists.

"What causes this?" Tally asked, politely, like a tourist who was also thinking of more interesting things.

"There must be a spring under the ground here. This is kind of Dancer's playground." The mud was criss-crossed with tire tracks and deep grooves where people got stuck.

"That's nice," she said woodenly.

He'd hurt her feelings. She was doing everything he wanted. She was being wild and taking chances. Look at that outfit!

And he was scared to death.

He switched his truck to four-wheel drive, put it in gear and aimed it at the center of the bog, a man driven to prove he was not afraid of anything. Somehow it had always seemed like so much fun before.

Now all he could think of was her shoulder touching his, the whiteness of her knuckles clutching the dash, the expression on her face.

The expression he had put there.

Okay, so he'd made a mistake, he could fix it now, right? They could have their picnic lunch up on the bank, and while Jed played with the dog, they could get dirty in the way she had interpreted it.

No they could not! She was Tally Smith. She'd never forgive herself or him if things got out of control in that way.

How did he get himself into these predicaments?

He got the truck out of the bog, retrieved a blanket from behind the seat and spread it out on the grass.

Of course Jed had been cooped up in the truck long enough and made straight for the bog. Tally settled herself on the blanket, removed a book from her bag and proceeded to ignore him.

J.D. followed Jed down to the bog. The little boy squatted at the edge, and J.D., being something of an expert on mud, took off his son's shoes and rolled up his pants past the knee.

"Look," J.D. said, and made a handprint in the mud. Then he made a footprint with Beau's paws.

In no time, Jed got the idea.

After they had done every kind of print except a face print, J.D. took his son's hand, and they strolled out in the mud, Jed laughing deliriously as the black gumbo sucked at his toes.

"What do you think you are doing?"

He turned around. Tally had put down her book—she must be past the *dirty* part—and she was standing at the edge of the bog, giving them her teacher-from-hell look.

"We're getting dirty. That's what boys are supposed to do."

"Grow up," she snapped. "It's filthy. Jed will get germs. I read about germs burrowing in the bottom of children's feet."

"You know how I feel about all your reading."

"Jed," she said sweetly, "come here. Auntie will get you cleaned up."

Jed looked at her mutinously. Obviously he had just begun exploring the joys of getting dirty. He wasn't nearly ready to give it up, to be cleaned up.

"Come on, Tally," J.D. said. "Instead of being the party pooper, come in. You'll like it. The mud squishing between your toes feels great."

"Oh," she said, miffed. "*I'm* the party pooper."

"It's not my fault that you misinterpreted what I meant about getting dirty. Honestly, you surprise me."

"I did not misinterpret you!"

"Oh, that's why you wore white to the mud bog. White and sexy. And by the way, sex is not dirty. Dirty is fun, mind you, but not that fun."

"This is an inappropriate conversation to be having in front of a four-year-old."

"How convenient for you. Take off your shoes. Roll up your pants. Come on."

"Never," she said.

"You know what, Tally Smith? Never is just the wrong word to say to a Turner." And what the hell? He really couldn't get much deeper into her bad books. He might as well have some fun.

"Come on, Jed," he said, using the little boy as a ruse and not feeling the least guilty about it. "Let's go see Auntie."

As soon as they got within snatching distance, he let go of the boy, and lunged for her. She turned, too late, to run, and he scooped her up in his arms.

Oh, God have mercy, he loved the sweet weight of her in his arms, the scent of her, the way her blouse was falling open and revealing the swell of her breast under the filmy fabric of that camisole.

"Put me down," she ordered, a schoolmarm who expected to be obeyed.

"Nope. I promised you dirty and dirty you're going to get."

"I'll scream."

"Scream away. No one to hear you."

He waded out into the bog. She clung to him very tightly. He took off her shoes one by one and threw them back on shore. Then he peeled off her socks. Her feet were dainty, and very white, and he wondered if she would think it was *dirty* if he kissed them. He resisted the impulse.

"Okay. I'm setting you down in it. Feel it."

"What if there's glass under there? Or twisted metal?"

"Or monsters," he said.

"These are my best slacks. J.D., they'll be wrecked."

"I'll buy you new ones." And some stainless steel appliances, too, if it keeps you from making the worst mistake of your life.

"Don't!" she shrieked, and tried to climb up him like he was a tree.

"Ooh," he said, "that feels good."

She went still, squinted at his face, and gave a little gasp of dismay. Then she wriggled out of his arms and landed feetfirst in the mud. "Ugh," she said. "This is awful. I hate this." And then a strange look came over her face.

"Pretty nice, isn't it?"

"No," she said.

"There go your ears again."

She closed her eyes, and lifted her feet and set them back down. "Oh my," she said, "Why didn't you tell me?"

Chapter Eight

Why hadn't J.D. told her this?

The mud was warm! Tally closed her eyes. The pleasure of the mud oozing up through her toes was almost unbearable. The temperature and texture of the mud reminded her of pudding that had been cooling on top of a stove.

She squeezed her toes, lifted a foot experimentally, and felt the powerful suck of the mud pulling on it.

She opened one eye to see J.D. studying her with a small smile on his face. It was hard enough to resist his looks when she managed to annoy him and he was scowling at her. But when he looked like this—his teeth flashing white, the sun glancing off the masculine perfection of his features, his eyes sparkling—the battle really felt like it was too much.

He had his jeans rolled up. She had already noticed the rip that exposed his knee and the worn threads across the behind that promised to expose more, given time. His shirt was open at the throat, and her eyes were drawn to the springy hairs of his chest, matched by the springy hairs on his calf muscles.

"I didn't tell you the spring running under the mud is a hot spring?" he asked innocently. "I could have sworn I mentioned that part."

"No, you forgot to tell me that part." She reached down and folded up the hem of her slacks, aware that he didn't mind her calf muscles either. The slacks folded up as high as she could get them, just below the knee, she stepped out a little deeper. The feeling of mud caressing her calf muscle was almost erotic. She wondered, fleetingly, what it would be like to take off all her clothes, and just give herself to the sensual pleasure of this strange, and wonderful place.

"I can't guarantee the germ content," J.D. said, as if it wasn't perfectly evident she was well and truly hooked.

"Sometimes," she said, and her voice was so strong and sure she wondered if it were even her own voice, "you just have to live dangerously."

"Dangewous," Jed echoed approvingly. She saw he was seated in the mud at the very edge of the bog busily building a leaning tower. Beauford was squeezed up against him, his nose tucked under Jed's arm. Beau's wrinkled face was stretched into an expression of complete adoration.

It tried to enter her mind that Jed was in his brand-new Child-of-the-Morning brand name overalls. Her white slacks were linen, not cheap either. Only J.D. looked as though he'd been truly prepared for this, in the worn jeans and old shirt. Still, he was not going to get off scott-free either. His truck was going to be a terrible mess when they all got back in it.

The thoughts, she realized, were penetrating her contentment, and so she swatted them away as though they were worrisome bugs.

She sighed as the warm mud pulled at her feet. She could not fight anymore. She just wanted to surrender to these feelings that kept surfacing from somewhere inside her. Tally did what she had started to do in the truck that day before it had spun out of control, what she had started to do under the stars last night before J.D.'s swift departure.

She let go.

She let go of plotting and worrying. She let go of her deep desire to get control back. She let go of thinking about the future and Herbert and the past and Elana.

She let go of her desire to act in a manner appropriate to a grade five teacher and the guardian of a four-year-old child.

She let go completely and let some part of her that wanted to be wild and free and unconventional pop its head out of the box she had kept it in all her life.

That part of her looked around at this brand-new world with grave curiosity. It sighed with happiness, excitement about all the things that were to be discovered and experienced and felt to the bottom of her toes. A newfound energy rippled through her, like laughter.

Swinging her arms, and watching her feet, she marched up and down through the mud, enjoying the simple pleasure of it slurping away at her toes, reveling in it.

And then she decided it was time to do something about the smirk on J.D.'s face. She knew what he was thinking. That it was a victory for him—that the uptight schoolmarm had finally let down her hair.

And that was true, but he might as well learn there was a price to be paid for such a victory.

She ducked, scooped up a handful of mud and lobbed

it at J.D. It caught him square in the chest, and a black blossom appeared on his shirt where she had hit him. She giggled at the look on his face—she had managed to shock and surprise him!

Giggled! Her, Tally Smith. Right under her picture in the high school yearbook it had said, "Girl least likely to giggle." Also, though it had not been written, least likely to shock or surprise anyone.

He stood there for a moment contemplating this development. He inspected the damage to his shirt very thoroughly before looking back up at her, cocking his head, studying her, his eyes as dark and brown and rich as the wet earth around them.

She stuck out her tongue at him.

And he lunged toward her. She could see the ridges of his thigh muscles standing out against the faded fabric of his jeans as he plunged through the mud. The sun glancing off hair on his arms, the play of his biceps were mesmerizing. She let the awareness she had of his utter masculinity fill her. It felt warm and oozing and delicious, just like the mud. He was almost on top of her before it occurred to her to move.

She broke out of her trance at just the right moment, and did the only thing she could do. She picked up more mud, flung it at him, and then turned tail and ran. Or approximated running. The mud sucked at her feet, slithered under her heels, threatened to pull her down. In no time she was breathless with exertion and laughter.

Jed was on the bank jumping up and down with excitement, chortling happily in the reflection of her joy.

And that's when she knew the gift she had to give her nephew.

Not safety. Not respectability.

The ability to embrace life and all the unexpected and

amazing surprises it threw at you. Her chest heaving, un-
ladylike sweat forming on her brow and under her arms,
she skidded to a halt, and spun to face her opponent.

She hunched over, rounded her shoulders, let her arms
hang loose at her sides.

He pulled up short and eyed her suspiciously. "What
is that? Your impression of Quasimodo?"

"It's a wrestling move," she told him indignantly.
"Bring it on."

He tilted back his head and laughed. She could see the
laughter gurgling up the strong column of his throat. It
was a rich and beautiful sound. She decided if freedom
had a sound, that is what it would sound like. J. D.
Turner's laughter.

And his face had an expression on it of discovery. His
eyes were dancing with laughter, his mouth was curved
into a smile that put the sun to shame. Taking his time,
and never taking his eyes off of her, J.D. scooped up a
big handful of mud. He tossed it back and forth between
his hands as he advanced on her.

She waited and before he had a chance to throw it, she
lunged at him, caught him around the knees and toppled
him. He went over like a giant tree falling, in slow motion.
The mud broke his fall, and spurted up on all sides of
them.

She went very still. The full length of J.D. was underneath her. Her chest touched his chest, and her stomach
touched his stomach and her legs were sprawled on top
of his legs.

The old Tally would have realized the position they
were in was suggestive, and would have squirmed to get
free, to get away from the sensations that were coursing
over her, like liquid fire.

"I think people pay for this, somewhere," the new

Tally murmured, as the mud enveloped them, tepid and heavy, a sensuous glove.

She made no attempt to move off of him. The mud was warm and exotically sensuous, but it had nothing on the warm and exotically sensuous lines of his body.

His arms went around her, pulling her yet closer to him, and the world stopped. The breeze stopped stirring the grass beside the bog. The birds stopped singing. Jed's excited crowing was a long way away.

The only movement in the world was the steady, strong beat of his heart right below her breast. She looked into the liquid brown of his eyes, breath stopped, hearts beating as one, for the longest time.

She was quite certain she might have been kissed if not for Jed and Beau entering the fray. Jed was pulling her off of J.D., pummeling her with soft mud balls. She allowed herself to be distracted, and pretending great fear of Jed, she took off running again. She slipped and fell, skidding headlong through the mud.

There was not an inch of her that was clean. The mud was in her hair and on her face. Grinning, J.D. came and offered her his hand.

"I saw a touchdown like that once. Last year's Super Bowl. The one your friend could have had tickets for."

She didn't really want to be reminded of her friend right now, and so she took his extended hand and yanked on it with all her might.

J.D. had been leaning forward to help her, and the unexpected direction of her momentum caught him off balance. He half turned and then toppled, plopping down in the mud beside her. When she started to struggle up he neatly caught her wrist, and then he and Jed teamed up, pelting mud at her while she tried to escape. Beauford was plunging frantic circles around them, until they were nearly all hysterical with laughter. She finally managed to gain her feet and get away.

J.D. swung Jed onto the broadness of his shoulders, tucked the sturdy little legs under his arms. "Hold on, pal."

"Get her," Jed yelled. "Giddy-up!"

It occurred to her she had never played with her nephew like this. Not down and dirty, no holds barred, playing. She had rarely seen him this boisterous.

She had read him storybooks and showed him board games. They listened to the best children's albums, Fred Penner and Raffi and Charlotte Diamond. He had several toy musical instruments and they played "house" with his molded plastic pint-size kitchen. They played with alphabet blocks and flash cards. They played hide-and-seek, and made tent houses under his bed. They had tea parties for the teddy bears and went to the park, where she walked beside him while he rode his trike down the quieter walkways. He went to play groups with children his own age and she took him on her school's field trips to museums and art galleries.

Until this very moment, Tally Smith would have claimed to have given her nephew the childhood out of a dream.

But this uncontrolled exuberance had never been part of their experience together.

She realized that it was the price she paid for being in control of her world, for wanting everything a certain way all the time.

And she realized, a little sadly, it was far too high a price to pay.

She glanced back at him, riding atop J.D.'s shoulders, and realized she had never seen him quite so happy. He shouted with joy! He glowed with it, his eyes shone, his teeth flashed small and white in the sun. He was covered in mud from his neck to his toes, and his overalls were ruined, and it didn't matter one little bit.

She danced a taunting circle, and in a burst of speed J.D. caught her. He caught her wrist and spun her around and she slipped and fell to her knees.

"Finally, got you where I want you," he said, swinging Jed off his shoulders. He put pressure on her shoulder until she was prone in the mud. And then they buried her, molding it around her until she was a sculpture of herself.

Her cheeks hurt from laughing so hard. She screamed with laughter, undignified, immature, giddy.

And when they were done molding her, they allowed her to come out of the mud with a giant slurp, and J.D. lay down.

To Beau's distress they buried J.D., too.

Oh, how she loved the excuse to touch him, packing mud around the muscles of his arms and broadness of his chest, piling it up on his legs.

"Hang on," she said, "let's make his arms a little bigger. Like Popeye, after he has the spinach."

"Something wrong with my arms the way they are?" J.D. growled.

"Well, yeah," she said. "They're, like, scrawny."

And then she screamed with laughter—undignified, immature and giddy—all over again.

When they were finished, he freed himself from the mud cake with disgusting ease and then they buried Jed.

Last but not least, they tried to get an unwilling Beauford. They chased the dog around the edges of the bog, slipping and sliding and falling and laughing.

And then, when Beau evaded them, they gave up and sat on the edges of the bog and built huge towers of mud, decorating them with handprints and footprints and drawings of stick men. Beau came back and they persuaded him to lend his paws to the designs on the towers of mud.

In all her life, Tally tried to think if she had ever felt this relaxed, this free, this herself. She tried to think if she had ever given herself so totally to the concept of having fun. And she knew she never had.

Fun had been a dangerous thing, something reserved for Elana. And there had always been a price to pay for it.

Casting a sidelong look at where J.D. sat, his eyebrows furrowed as he carved into the side of a mud castle, she knew it was because of him.

Not just because he had forced her to accompany him to this place.

No, it was not so much about the mud bog as about him. She had the feeling that going to the store for a carton of milk was something he could make fun. The truth was he made her heart want to sing. Just being around him made her feel alive and happy and she just didn't have the strength to fight it anymore.

She didn't know what the future held. Herbert, presumably. But she could grasp what today held, and feel the fullness of her heart and the laughter in her belly.

And those things inside her, like nourishment, forever.

Finally, exhausted they lay back in the sun on the bank of the mud bog, side by side with Jed and Beau squeezed between them.

Jed was soon fast asleep, his chest rising and falling contentedly. Beauford's head rested on his tummy.

As the mud dried on her, J.D. reached across and chipped a little piece off her face. "Penny for your thoughts."

"Inflation," she said. "I need a buck."

He fished in jeans that had become too tight now that

they were wet and muddy. "Canadian, okay?" he said, handing her the gold coin that was the Canadian dollar.

She inspected it, pretended to bite it and then put it in her pocket. "I was thinking my clothes are ruined," she said.

"Liar."

"And that your truck is going to be a real mess."

"Still lying."

"Oh, how do you know? And don't tell me my ears and nose are glowing, because they are covered under several layers of revolting black slime."

He touched her brow, moved a dirty strand of hair off her forehead. "When you worry you get these little wrinkles up here. You don't have them right now. For someone covered in several layers of revolting black slime, you look distinctly happy, Tally Smith."

She sighed. "I hope that's worth a buck. Because that's all there is. I'm happy."

"And you haven't been happy enough in your life, have you?"

She glanced at him. Who had ever cared about the happiness in her life before? She didn't lean on people. They leaned on her. She didn't tell people her problems, they told her theirs. And so she was slightly amazed to find herself telling him about the challenges that had come from being Elana's sister.

"I always thought," she finished sadly, "if I let go— if I was silly, or immature—I'd end up like her. Out of control. Crazy. My life blown apart, the messy debris of what used to be scattered from here to kingdom come."

"There was a certain beauty to her craziness," he said softly. "Maybe you could keep the best parts and leave the rest."

"There was a beauty to it, wasn't there?" she said.

He nodded.

It was his forgiveness of her sister even though she had hurt him, left him without a goodbye, never told him about his son, that made the tears sting behind Tally's eyes.

"Well, it's all over now," she said, trying to fight back the tears.

"How can it be over when you miss her so? When you have her son. Let it out, Tally. Just let those feelings out."

Feelings were all to be controlled, good ones and bad ones. But the new Tally allowed herself to sniffle. "I miss her so. There was no one quite like Elana when she was in a good mood."

"I know that," he said quietly. "I saw her like that. Vital and full of life and enthusiasm. She walked in a room and it was as if the light turned on."

"Are you sorry you loved her?" Tally asked.

He gazed thoughtfully at the sky, and then looked over at her. He traced the line of her cheek with his finger.

"For the longest time, I was bitter, and very angry. It really hurt me when she left. We didn't know each other very long, but I just thought she was going to be the one. Because of the way she made me feel—alive and bold and like anything in the whole world was possible."

For a lovely moment, Tally felt like her sister, at her best, was right there with them. How she would have loved the mud and the laughter they had just shared.

"She didn't even say goodbye, she just packed up her stuff and disappeared. I guess that was the moment I decided a life of blissful bachelorhood was for me."

Tally wanted desperately to tell him that he couldn't remain a bachelor forever. She had watched him with Jed. She could see the gift he had to give to a family of his own.

But if she said that, it felt like it would be encouraging him to marry anyone. And she didn't want that. Couldn't bear it. He was going to be part of Jed's life forever. So, how would she feel when he came visiting with his girl-friend, his wife?

She would feel sick with jealousy, that's how she would feel. The old Tally would never have allowed herself such a petty emotion.

But the new Tally knew something the old one didn't.

She went very still.

He said, slowly, "I don't feel angry at her anymore, Tally. I feel like I'm part of something bigger than myself, a bigger plan. I have a son. I met you. Because of her. For the first time in my whole life, I'm looking around me with the certainty that everything is exactly as it is meant to be."

His words, his humble awe in the face of the miracle of forgiveness he had found in himself, only underscored the feeling she was harboring for him, the secret she had just learned about herself.

Her stillness registered on him, and he turned and looked at her quizzically. He whistled low in his throat.

"I'll pay more than a buck for that one," he said, softly.

But this thought she wasn't sharing. It felt like she couldn't breathe, let alone speak. The terrifying truth had just come to her.

She loved him. She had fallen totally and hopelessly in love with J. D. Turner. When had that happened? How could that have happened?

Tally Smith could not do something as impetuous as fall for a man she had just met. Or the old Tally couldn't.

The new one realized from the first time she had looked at his picture, she had felt the irresistible pull of him.

Some part of her had known he was the man who could save her from herself, and that part had drawn her in search of him.

In search of her own heart.

"Well," she said, sitting up, and smiling brightly, "it must be time to go."

"Don't do that, Tally," he said in a low voice.

"What?"

"Don't go back to being her again."

"Who?"

"You know. That fake you that you hold out to the world because you're so damned scared that if you cut loose you won't survive. You're not your sister. It's better for Jed if you can be free and natural and yourself."

Jed. A reminder that her life was going to be linked with this man's for a long, long time. A long time to live with humiliation if she told him how she felt, and he laughed. No, he wouldn't laugh. It would be worse than laughter. He'd be gentle and sympathetic. Their relationship would always have this embarrassing complication in it.

"I don't know what you're talking about. Look at the mess." She chipped some mud off the sleeve of a blouse that would never be white again.

"Please don't," he said.

But what choice did she have? Admit the humiliating truth? That she had given up control to fall hopelessly and helplessly in love?

Was there any possibility he could feel the same way? Of course not. He was the charter member of the Dancer, North Dakota, A.G.M.N.W.N.C. And if he ever gave up his membership, it probably wouldn't be for a girl like her.

He leaned toward her, and cupped his hand behind her

head. She knew she should pull away, that she was already in way over her head. She knew that, and yet she greedily wanted every moment he would give her.

He pulled her toward him. Over the top of the sleeping boy and the dog, their lips met.

All the control she had tried so hard all her life to have, evaporated, just like that. Gone. Because she took the fullness of his lips and gently gnawed it between her teeth. She savored the taste of him, she felt her own lips part at the gentle insistence of his tongue.

His tongue explored the contours of her mouth, and then it stroked her earlobes and the hollow of her throat and then it went back to her mouth.

And then her tongue did some exploring of its own. Until they were both panting with want, both of them unleashing that which had been leashed.

Desire.

Passion.

And the scariest thing of all. Hope.

He was losing himself in her. He wanted her more than he had wanted any woman, ever. Her lips were full and sweet, and right underneath the sweetness sizzled something more; more powerful, more frightening, more everything.

Tally Smith, uptight and prim, was a woman beautiful enough to inspire fantasy. But Tally Smith, with her hair down, with her clothing molded to her, with mud streaking her face, with her amazing eyes sparking with mischief, was simply irresistible.

He told himself *whoa*. But it was like a horse who'd finally been allowed to run after too much time in a stall. The whoa button was not working.

He knew he needed to think about this.

Long. Hard. Carefully. His life was going to be tangled with hers until his son was an adult.

Could they risk a complication like this?

Could they stop it?

It didn't seem like either of them could stop it. Thankfully, Jed picked that moment to stir sleepily, to look up at them with puzzled eyes, before he closed them again.

J.D. reared back from her, looked at her astonished and disoriented. Every kiss seemed to deepen his desire to kiss her, rather than slake it.

He came face-to-face with his own arrogance. All this time he'd been so certain what a woman should know.

But how could he know what a woman should know? He suddenly wasn't even certain what a man should know!

He ran a hand through his hair. "You know what? We should get out of these clothes before they're glued to us."

And then he blushed. He could feel it moving up his neck like a brick-red tide, and he couldn't believe it. Under his picture in the old high school annual didn't it say "Boy least likely to ever blush"?

"I didn't mean it like that," he said.

"Like what?" she asked, innocently.

"I just meant we should head over to my place. We'll shower. I mean not together or anything." He could feel the blush deepening.

She was smiling at him, a smile that said she already knew every damn thing she needed to. But he didn't have his list with him. If he consulted his list maybe he could get back on track, remember what the hell came after the lesson on germs and getting dirty.

Both of which she had mastered. She was an "A" student. They could be crossed off the list, no more practice needed. Thank God. Anymore practicing getting dirty with her and there was really no telling what would happen.

He started talking again, way too fast.

"You can throw on some of my clothes and we'll put our stuff in the washer and barbecue some steaks for dinner or something. We could rent a movie if you wanted."

It sounded like he was asking her for a date. Well, okay, that's what he was doing. He was asking her for a date.

He was going to cook her dinner and watch a movie with her. And maybe hold her hand, and maybe kiss her again.

It depended. Maybe once he found his list, he could get back on track, bring this mission back under control, complete it successfully.

Though J. D. Turner was no longer nearly as certain as he once had been what that meant.

Chapter Nine

They arrived at his house, and J.D. ushered them in, taking a surreptitious look on the kitchen table for his list. He frowned. It wasn't there. Maybe on the counter. He frowned at the counter, too. The list wasn't there, but the engine was.

"You two have the bathroom first," he said, gallantly. That would give him a chance to find his list, and get the engine off the counter.

"Have you got something I can wear?"

He looked at her and smiled. Tally looked like she had been carved in mud. Her clothes, black now, were molded to her body. And an exquisite body it was.

The thought of her wearing his clothes chased the thought of the list and the engine right out of his head.

"I'm sure I can find something for you to throw on." He went into his bedroom, which looked like disaster had struck. A few days of clothes were on the floor, the sheets were a rumpled tangle, and the comforter was on the floor where he left it in the summer because Beau liked to sleep on it.

He momentarily forgot the clothes and started making the bed. Then he drew himself up short. What was he making the bed for? She wasn't coming in here! He whirled from the bed, aware of little clumps of mud flying off of him every time he moved. Clothes, he reminded himself.

Presumably clean would be better.

He opened his closet, and found her his newest pair of jeans on a hanger. He always hung his jeans up fresh out of the dryer because then they didn't need to be ironed. The jeans were nearly new and clean and obviously were going to swim on her.

And he was probably going to have to give them to the thrift store after she'd worn them because the thought of her skin being inside the same fabric as his skin was going to create constant problems. Especially since there was the distinct possibility she would not be wearing underwear inside that fabric. Not that he wanted his mind to go there.

But since it had, he should be practical. If he was getting rid of the jeans after, maybe he should give her an older pair. He threw the newer pair on the floor, and picked out an older pair, which was a few threads short in the rear.

Considering the conclusion he had reached about her underwearless state, the threadbare jeans would not do. His whole collection of jeans ended up on the floor, and he finally opted for the new pair.

"Is everything okay?" she called. "It doesn't have to fit. I'll just tie up the pants with a string or something."

"Everything's fine." She was going to tie the pants up with a string, like one of those hillbilly girls in *Lil' Abner*.

The intense heat of that thought made him realize he had to renew his search for the list.

He took a quick look for it while he was searching for something she could tie the pants up with. The list was not on top of his bureau, under his bed or underneath his pillow, and neither was anything to hold up the pants.

"J.D.," she called, "if you don't have anything, we can go back to the motel. It will just take a few minutes."

But he didn't want her to go back to the motel. Once she was back there, she might come to her senses, or he might come to his. But wasn't that why he was trying to find the list? So that he could review his goals? Stick with the game plan? Come to his senses? It was not on that list to kiss her until they were both giddy from it, he knew that. But on the other hand, he was committed to a course of not allowing her to become a dried-up prune.

"J.D.?"

"No, no, I have lots of clothes."

He reminded himself he was being gallant, so he grabbed the new pair of jeans, and his best belt, which would need additional holes punched in it.

Then he opened his bureau and scowled at his T-shirts, sort of hoping the list would materialize among them, and sort of glad when it didn't. He not only had lots of T-shirts, he had way too many.

For instance, did you give her the T-shirt that said Snow Removal by Chris, and in brackets We Blow Big Time. No, absolutely not. He tossed that one on the floor.

Stan gave him a T-shirt almost every year for Christmas. Gifts were a tricky thing among the members of the A.G.M.N.W.N.C. Nothing too sentimental would do, and a few years ago Stan had discovered T-shirts as the ideal macho-type gift. Most of Stan's selections J.D. had never worn, because you didn't want to spoil a perfectly good new T-shirt pulling wrenches when you already had a dozen shirts with holes in them or grease stains on them.

That would be good—giving her a brand-new T-shirt. Very classy. It would look like he just kept a spare T-shirt around all the time. For company.

Which maybe, come to think of it, was not quite the impression he wanted to give.

But when he looked over the Stan collection of fine T-shirt apparel, he remembered that maybe them being new wasn't the only reason he hadn't worn them. One was a souvenir shirt from a place called Boobers. It joined Snow Removal by Chris on the floor. Then there was the one with a woman's body in a bikini, but the neck joined the wearer's neck, something like those wooden photo stand-ups where you put your head through the hole. Several were not nearly as tasteful as the first two.

Tally was not ready for Stan's sense of humor. They joined the others on the floor. He had seen her in that awful purple sweater, and knew purple was definitely not her color, so the plain purple shirt ended up on the floor, too.

With relief, he finally found a plain white T-shirt at the bottom of the drawer.

However, if her bra was dirty and he had to assume it was, she wouldn't be wearing that piece of underwear, either. Her nipples were going to show through it, and that would be as bad as having her in the house with the jeans that were a little worn through in the rear. He tossed the white one on the floor, too.

He found a navy blue T-shirt that only had a little emblem over the left breast, for the Dancer Volunteer Fire Department. You weren't supposed to wear them except for official fire hall duties, but he figured this was an emergency as real as any the fire department had dealt with in recent history.

He opened the door and shoved the clothes out to her before she could glimpse in and see the mess his room was in.

He closed the door before she could say thanks.

Now something for him. The great thing about being a bachelor was that you could get dressed in the dark. You didn't have to—

"Have you got a T-shirt I could slip onto Jed while I wash his clothes?"

The white one would do for Jed. J.D. opened the door a crack and shoved it out at her. Who could have imagined this when he'd answered his door a very few nights ago in a towel? That he would be making wardrobe decisions considerably more complicated than the one he had made that night? He should have never answered the door.

But since he had, he had. He kicked through the T-shirts, frowning at the selection and finally stopped himself dead. What was he doing?

He was acting like a teenage boy going to the prom. Which he had been once, and he remembered he and his father trying to figure out the protocol for the evening. A kindly neighbor lady had come to his rescue, lending him the suit her older son had worn a year or two previously.

But there was no neighbor lady now, and he felt that same need for rescue. He despised himself for acting as if his choice of T-shirt mattered. The truth was he had a limited time to get that engine off the counter!

Whether it is getting that engine off the counter or selecting exactly the right T-shirt, you are trying to impress Tally Smith, a voice inside his head warned him.

He wished he had more time to contemplate what that meant, but he heard the water turn on in the bathroom, and felt he was in a race against time to get the engine off the kitchen counter.

Still, something defiant in him had to answer that accusing voice in his head, so just to prove he didn't give a damn what she thought he chose the Boobers shirt. At the last minute he turned it inside out so that Tally wouldn't notice the emblem and reach the erroneous conclusion he had ever been in the restaurant chain that featured waitresses with large chests. Even he was not enough of a chauvinist to think that would be entertaining.

He'd leave on the muddy jeans until after his own shower. He went out of his room. He could hear Jed splashing merrily in the tub, her voice moving around his like a melody. He wasted precious moments listening to them, letting the warmth of their voices wrap around him like the peach-colored light of early morning.

Then he charged into the kitchen, telling himself the whole way that moving the engine wasn't about impressing her either. He tried to think what it was about, but didn't come up with anything satisfactory, and he had a more immediate problem to solve anyway. What to do with the engine? Moving it all the way out to the shop would be a bigger job than he had time for.

He opened the cupboard door under the sink, and took out the garbage can. He lifted the engine, grunting under the weight of it, and shoved it under the sink. The cupboard door wouldn't quite close, and the garbage can was now in the middle of the floor, but the counter space was improved.

Was that the bathroom door squeaking open? He heard the banshee yell of Jed freed, looked at the garbage can, opened his oven door and jammed the garbage can into the oven. The oven door didn't quite close, either, but it was hardly noticeable.

J.D. grabbed a scouring pad and was trying to get the grease off the counter when Jed erupted into the room, tripping over the white T-shirt that swam around him. Beauford skittered along the floor behind him, as dirty as ever.

J.D. heard the tub draining, and the shower turning on. So, he still had a few minutes. Not enough time to order stainless steel appliances obviously, but enough to change into the purple T-shirt.

No way. The insanity stopped here. He had a few minutes to be with his son, and that was what he was going to do.

"Hey buddy," he said, picking him up and setting him down on his newly cleaned counter. "All clean?"

"Yup. Aw cwean. Baf Beaufewd?"

"Um, well bathing Beauford is not something to be undertaken casually." It was not something to be undertaken at all if you were trying to make your kitchen pass muster, since the only place it was possible to control the dog was in the kitchen sink.

"Pwee?"

Well, who could resist that? Besides this nonsense about trying to impress Tally just had to stop. J.D. had a right to be himself. He was a bachelor! That meant the dog got bathed in the kitchen sink.

Besides, his son wanted to bathe the dog. How could he refuse one of the first direct requests Jed had made of him?

"Beauford," he called. "Come here, boy."

Beauford, whose instincts were so finally honed he usually could not be found at bathtime, skulked toward him, aware something was up.

"That's love," J.D. told the dog as he scooped him up,

and wedged him into the sink. "It gets you into hot water before you even know what happened."

The dog was so in love with the kid, he couldn't think straight. He just sat there as they ran the water around him, not wriggling or whining or doing any of his normal highly effective escape maneuvers.

It occurred to J.D. that Beauford was not the only male in the house not thinking straight. Because he wasn't using any of his own repertoire of highly effective escape maneuvers, either. What kind of member of A.G.M.N.W.N.C. was he, hiding his engines and searching for the right outfit?

The Ain't Gettin' Married, No Way, Never Club suddenly seemed highly juvenile, a ridiculous creation of two men dying of loneliness and afraid to admit it.

By the time Tally emerged from the bathroom, J.D.'s only job was to keep a light hand on Beauford's collar while Jed lovingly scooped bubbles onto the dog's head. It was a testament to his newfound love that Beauford was so easy to hold. It usually took all of J.D.'s muscle, a couple of C-clamps and three bungee cords to keep the dog in the sink.

Jed worked a facecloth into every wrinkle and between each toenail.

"What's this?" Tally asked.

J.D. turned and looked at her. No underwear. You could tell even through the navy blue shirt.

She looked absolutely gorgeous, her hair towel-rumpled and curling, her face pink and scrubbed from the shower. She should have looked like a scarecrow in those too large clothes, but she didn't.

She had the shirt tied in a knot above her belly button, and the belt tied in a knot around her waist. The jeans were rolled up to the knee and her feet were bare. She looked just like one of those hillbilly girls. J.D. had the evil thought she would look nice laying down in a haystack, or a meadow filled with yellow wildflowers. Or in his bed.

She would look damned nice lying down anywhere.

As long as she was waiting for him. It was A.G.M.N.W.N.C. treason to think such a thought, but J.D. thought it anyway, and to hell with the A.G.M.N.W.N.C.

She looked relaxed and happy, like a girl who knew how to have fun. She came across the kitchen and in a second was up to her elbows in suds, laughing at Beauford's woebegone expression.

When had that happened? She liked his dog!

That was it. J.D. was officially retiring from the club. And he wasn't looking for that ridiculous list anymore, either.

She's hell-bent on marrying someone else, J. D. Turner. Yeah? Well, we'll just see about that.

He felt himself go very still. Over the sounds of the water slopping and Jed and Tally laughing, he could hear the beat of his own heart.

And it seemed to be spelling out her name.

He'd only ever felt this way once before. With Elana Smith. This way, only different, too. With Elana the excitement had sizzled in the air, nonstop, vaguely exhausting. They had pursued the *things* that made them feel that way: clubs, eating out, car races, sex.

For the first time he understood much of the excitement between Elana and him had been generated by events outside of themselves.

And that was what felt so totally different this time.

The feeling of well-being was deep and good, and it came from inside of him. From his heart. It was the most genuine thing he had ever felt.

He was falling in love with Tally Smith.

In a daze, he turned from the quizzical look on her face and turned on the oven. Tonight, he would dazzle her. He'd cook her dinner and they'd put Jed to bed, and hold hands and exchange kisses.

And maybe he would tell her about this funny feeling in his chest and his heart.

Or maybe not.

He turned his attention to the menu. He'd grill steaks, which he was good at. And he considered baked potatoes one of his most notable culinary accomplishments. He had stuff for salad, and ice cream for dessert—

"J.D., there seems to be smoke coming out of your oven."

He came out of his reverie, and looked at the thick black smoke curling out of the burners and the slightly ajar oven door.

The garbage can! He leapt across the kitchen and threw open the oven door, enveloping them all in a cloud of thick black smoke. The smoke detector started to squeal.

Beauford, no dummy, leapt from the sink, and headed for the door, trailing a wide swatch of bubbles behind him.

Fifteen minutes later, once the garbage can and Beauford had both been hosed off, they all sat in J.D.'s backyard beside the melted blackened garbage can and watched the sun go down.

Tally sat on the grass, Beauford wrapped in a blanket on her lap.

She had braved the smoke-filled kitchen to go back in the house and get a blanket for the dog. She wasn't pretending. She really liked his dog!

"Okay," she said, quietly, "enough. I want to know why the garbage was in the oven, and why there is an engine sticking out from under your sink causing a hazard to anyone with shins, and why you have that horrible Boobers T-shirt on inside out.''

He went very still, for the second time in less than an hour. A million things came to his mind, but not one of them came out. He looked at his foot.

''I better go have my shower now.''

''Not until you answer the question.''

He glowered at her. She wanted to know? Okay, he'd tell her. ''The embarrassing fact is, Tally Smith, I seem to be doing my damnedest to impress you. And I'd say, from the smoke still billowing out the kitchen window, that I'm doing a poor job of it.''

She touched him. She leaned toward him. She smelled like a wet dog and plastic-y smoke. ''The embarrassing fact is, John David Turner, that you did that a long time ago, without even half-trying.''

He stared at her. She looked back at him, long and level.

He cleared his throat. ''Well, I'll just go have that shower now.''

''You do that. I'll be here when you get out.''

That's what I'm afraid of.

Tally did a little jig around the backyard. When she saw Jed staring at her, she took his hands and jigged around with him. The dog wriggled out of his blanket and leaped ecstatically around them.

''He's trying to impress *me*,'' she said told her nephew. ''He likes me.''

It had never felt like this with Herbert. Never. They *did* things. They had had dinner in the finest restaurants in Saskatchewan. They had gone to live theater, and charity balls. They *collected* things like those stainless steel appliances.

But they didn't *feel* things.

Here she was happy, with a stinky wet dog jumping on her, and smoke pouring out the kitchen, and the blackened remains of a garbage can beside her.

The bathroom window was open, and she could hear J.D. singing.

Oh, he had the most terrible voice when he shouted his song like that, and yet she was not sure she had ever heard such a delightful noise.

So, she and Jed and the dog danced, to the sounds of "Annabel was a cow of unusual bovine beaut*eeee*...."

She finally collapsed in the grass, hugging herself, while the dog and the child continued to celebrate the magic that tingled in the air around them.

There was a wonderful excitement in her, a sense of the world being brand-new and open to all kinds of possibilities. It had just never been like this in her whole life.

After she had enjoyed her hug for a few seconds, she shut the gate on the small yard and gave Jed and Beauford strict instructions they were not to leave. Beauford looked like he got it, and like he would defend Jed with his last breath if he had to.

Then she braved the kitchen. It stank! Still, J.D. had taken steaks out, and they were thawing in the microwave. In the top cupboard she found a little box of candles labeled Emergency Road Candles, and since she couldn't find candleholders, she melted them onto saucers and scattered them around the kitchen.

She went back outside and picked wild grass and daisies and tiny, dainty flowers she didn't recognize, and brought them in the house and put them in a water pitcher.

J.D. came out of the shower, as she was lighting the candles. "Wow. What's this all about?"

Embracing life. Trusting the universe. Believing in mir-

acles. Whatever it was about was too big for words, even with her vocabulary, so she just shrugged.

They took the steaks back outside and lit the barbecue and took turns turning steaks and chasing the boy and the dog.

They snuck looks at each other, and smiled silly smiles and their hands touched more often than was necessary.

I'm falling more in love by the second, she thought, *and I can't get enough of it.* Jed was asleep before supper was halfway done, and J.D. picked him up in his arms and carried him through to his spare room, tucked the covers carefully around him. Beauford jumped up on the bed, sighed, and put his head between his paws.

They finished dinner, trading stories about high school insecurities until her face hurt from laughing.

"I'll do the dishes," she said, when they were done.

"Nah. I'll just throw them in the oven, and do them next week. The sink will need to be sterilized before I use it again, anyway."

"J. D. Turner, you're talking as if that dog has germs," she scolded lightly.

He laughed. She liked making him laugh. She thought she liked it best of all, until he said to her, his voice a low growl, "You ever been much of a dancer, Tally Smith?"

"No," she said, shaking her head. "Hated it. Felt self-conscious."

"Well, we can't have you leaving Dancer feeling that same way, can we?"

Leaving. She registered the word, but refused to hear it. For once in her pathetic life she was going with her heart, not her head.

He led her into the living room, taking the candles with

them. It was a plain room, with plain furniture and a hard-wood floor, no rug.

But the candles and the look on his face transformed it into a ballroom. He turned, selected a CD and put it on his stereo.

"That's not the type of music I would have expected you to have," she said as the soft sounds of a beautiful female voice filled the room. J.D. opened his arms and she went into them, felt them close around her.

The sensation of homecoming was fierce, and she decided it wasn't making him laugh that she liked best of all. It was being with him, just like this, their bodies pressed together, his breath stirring the hair on the top of her head.

"Don't tell Stan," he folded her tighter against him, "He thinks the only music I own is country and old time rock and roll."

Stan, another member of that bachelor club J.D. was so fond of. But again, she would not allow her head to go there. It was trying so hard to mess with her heart.

"Your secret is safe with me," she murmured.

"Why do I have a feeling all my secrets would be safe with you," he said, his lips stirring the hair on the crown of her head.

And then the words stopped between them and they just swayed to the gentle, soaring notes of a beautiful song.

She melted into him, feeling his strength, his hand on the small of her back, the heat of his thigh where it touched hers. This couldn't be right. She was engaged to someone else. This couldn't be right at all.

And yet, she could not think of a time that had felt more right for her, ever.

The stars rose in the sky outside the living room window. The CD changed and the sound of a lone flute filled the room.

J.D. began to sing. And not about Annabel the cow, either. His voice deep and gravelly, rough with feeling, he sang a song about a warrior who had left the one he loved behind, who lay on a bed of rocky ground the night before the battle, thinking of the green fields of home and the green eyes of his lady lover.

"If he dies," she whispered, "I am going to cry."

And of course, the warrior died, and she cried.

J.D. lifted her tears on a gentle fingertip to his lips, and licked it. "My singing always makes people cry," he teased.

"Where did you learn that song?"

"My mother sang it sometimes, she sang it as though her heart were breaking." And then he told her about his mother.

She knew he had just given her the gift of his complete trust, and it was as if she could feel the air in the room changing around them, becoming as warm as an embrace, tingling with promise, glowing with the soft hopes of two people who had lost their ability to hope somewhere along the way.

After a long time, he kissed her, but gently. He whispered, "I'm afraid of what happens next, Tally Smith."

"What happens next?" she said huskily.

And he kissed her again. It was not like any other kiss they had shared. The barriers were completely gone between them. It was as if their souls had melted together, and nothing was left to separate them.

His kiss was tender and exquisite and welcoming.

He guided her over to the couch, and they sat down. He broke the kiss but held her tight.

"Lord," he murmured, "help me be the man I need to be."

She reached for his lips, but he touched hers with his finger, shook his head slightly. "No more. Tonight, just let me hold you."

She snuggled against him, aware of the rich feeling of contentment within her, aware of having never in her entire life felt this good, this at peace, this connected to another human being. He wrapped his arms tight around her, pulled her into him, rested his chin on her hair, kissed the crown of her head.

And she slept.

In the morning she woke up alone and the aloneness made her feel frightened, lonely in a way she had never felt before.

Because she had never allowed herself to feel so completely trusting, to lean so hard on another person as she had come to lean on J.D.

She heard giggles from the kitchen and her sensation of being frightened and alone evaporated. She tiptoed to the doorway. Morning light was spilling in the window. J.D. and Jed were at the kitchen table slurping Popsicles, and Beauford was at his bowl eating his own blue one.

They all looked up at her, guilty.

"I know it's not the breakfast of champions," J.D. said.

"Who cares? What flavors do you have left?"

"Cherry and lime. Beauford got the last blue one."

"Not lime," she said, and held out her hand for the cherry one. She sat down at the table. She was in someone else's clothes, in someone else's house, she was rumpled and crumpled, and her hair was most certainly a mess.

She bit into the cherry Popsicle and decided she had never been happier.

"I guess I should put my clothes in the dryer," she

said. "I got distracted last night and didn't take them out of the washer."

"Really?" he said innocently.

She gave him a little punch and he howled in pretended pain until Jed was screeching with laughter.

His washer and dryer were in a little room by the back door, and she went there.

It felt so…domestic, somehow, settled.

She took her clothes out of the washer. They were ruined, of course. They would never come clean again. She should probably just put them in the garbage.

Or save them.

For memories.

Better yet, for future trips to the mud bog.

Her and Jed's clothes looked after, she noticed that the clothes J.D. had worn yesterday were in a heap on the floor.

It increased that feeling of being settled when she picked them up to throw them in the washer for him. It was a little like playing house.

She closed her eyes for a moment, and imagined this was her life.

The boy and the man eating breakfast, her putting a load of laundry in, the laughter ringing, the love singing throughout the house.

A silly fantasy, she thought, opening her eyes. Out of long habit, she checked the pockets of J.D.'s jeans before she put them in the washer.

There was three dollars and some change in the front right pocket, a dog biscuit and several rubber washers in the left one.

In the back pocket was a piece of paper, folded, the mud had nearly ruined it. She wondered if it was important, or just something she could toss in the garbage.

She unfolded it, and through the streaks of mud, she saw masculine spiky handwriting, and the words What a Woman Should Know.

Frowning slightly, she read all about what J. D. Turner thought a woman should know.

His list might have been funny, if it hadn't been so insulting. The list made it apparent what he really thought of her: that she was so superficial she'd put appliances ahead of her heart, that she was too uptight to raise a child properly, that left to her own devices she would end up a dried prune of a woman.

Nothing that had happened between them had been spontaneous at all. It had all been part of a plan to change her into something more palatable to him, someone more worthy of raising his son.

She had made a grave mistake. She had trusted J. D. Turner. She had let go of control. Her whole life experience had tried to tell her that both trust and loss of control were harbingers to disaster. She realized that if she was going to survive this with even a shred of her dignity intact, she had to leave and she had to leave now.

Chapter Ten

J.D. knew as soon as he looked at her face that something was terribly wrong. It wasn't the same as that pinched look she got when she let go, and then pulled back, and then let go again. It wasn't the same as that at all.

In fact, Tally was trying to smile bravely, but the smile did not reach her eyes. Her eyes held a terrible wound in them.

"I've decided," she said brightly, "that you and Jed need some time together. Without me. To bond. So you can tell him the truth."

"I can tell him the truth right now," he said. "Ten seconds."

He went down on one knee, in front of his son's chair. He gently wiped some of the bright orange Popsicle ring from around his child's mouth. "Jed, I have something to tell you. I'm your Daddy. I didn't know about you for a long, long time, but now that I do, it's about the happiest thing that ever happened to me."

Jed flung his arms around J.D.'s neck and J.D. felt a little trickle of melting Popsicle going down his spine. "Daddy," Jed whispered in his ear. "I always wanted a daddy."

J.D. felt the rise and fall of his son's chest, the beat of his heart against his own. Then Jed reared back, and looked at him, his eyes wide and round. "Is Beau my bwudda?"

J.D. might have laughed, celebrated how momentous an occasion this was by bringing out another round of Popsicles, except for the look on her face. The pain there made J.D. set his Popsicle down and get up, move toward her.

"All the same," she said backing toward the door, "I'm going to go. I need some time to myself."

"Tell me what happened," he said, reaching out and touching the now familiar curve of her shoulder with the palm of his hand. She flinched, and he frowned and took his hand away.

"Nothing happened. I just feel mixed up. I'm marrying another man."

But it was deeper than that, and he watched her face carefully for clues, at the same time as answering, firmly, "No, you aren't."

"Yes, I am!" A little temper starting to show, which was better than the sadness that was darkening her eyes to a shade of pitch. She looked for all the world like someone had up and died on her.

"Let me tell you something," he said, and then tried for the gentle approach, "and sorry if it hurts, but it's the truth and you need to hear it. That man is not very interested in marrying you, not now and not ever."

She stiffened as if he had slapped her.

"Nothing personal, I'm sure," he added hastily. "You just aren't very well suited."

"And you are the expert on what suits me for what reason?"

"Come on Tally, I've seen you playing in the mud. That makes me a bit of an expert." When she looked unconvinced, he admitted, "Besides, I talked to Herbert about it. I don't think there are wedding bells in your future. At least not with him."

"You talked to him about our wedding? When?"

From the little edge of hysteria in her voice, J.D. realized telling her that may have been a small tactical error.

"I gave him a call the other night. Just to chat. You know, since you had led me to believe he was going to be a significant other in my child's life. Soon. You'd set a date, were your exact words. But he said you hadn't."

"I never said we set a date. I said we were going to set a date. And you phoned Herbert? And talked about me?"

"I just asked about the wedding plans. That's all. And I didn't get the impression he was really excited. You know, Tally, the man who marries you should be excited about it. Really excited." He could feel his own heartbeat move into double time at the thought of being the one lucky enough to marry Tally Smith.

"Just because he doesn't show his excitement in the same way as you, does not mean he is not excited. We can't all be Neanderthals."

If J.D. was really an Neanderthal, he'd grab her by her hair and take her back to his cave. But the flat light in her eyes required sensitivity. Not his specialty.

"Tally, don't be dumb."

"I'm marrying him," she said with ferocious resolve. "And I am not turning into an old prune because of it. In fact, I am going to be happy. Deliriously happy with my stainless steel appliances, and my rules, and my lack of germs. I am going to be happy with a life of lovely cleanliness, that unfolds predictably, without ugly surprises."

He had a sinking feeling in his gut. The worst possible thing had happened. The opposite side had found the battle plan.

Only she didn't feel like the opposing side anymore, and it hadn't felt like a battle for a long time. Not until just this moment, and now it felt like he was battling for his life.

Which is what he should have said. Instead he blurted out, "You found my list! Where was it? I spent the better part of yesterday looking for it."

It sounded like an accusation, and he realized it was another tactically poor move because of the look of deepening hurt on her face.

"It was in your back jean pocket. And you were looking for it why? So you could check my progress? Give me a report card?"

"Tally, it wasn't like that." It had been in his back pocket the whole time? Geez, if he had found it, he wouldn't be in this awful predicament.

Maybe if he'd found it in time, he could have avoided the falling in love with her part, and stuck to the plan and completed his mission successfully.

Missed the falling in love with her part? But that had been the best part.

"Tally," he said, firmly, strongly, "my feelings for you are real."

"Your feelings for me? Which me? From the very beginning you wanted to change me into something I never was. You wanted me to be free and wild. I bet you told yourself it was for Jed's sake didn't you?"

"Well yes, but—"

"Was it fun for you? Playing with me? Practicing your warped form of behavior modification on me? It must have been a real laugh for you when you saw me coming around, becoming exactly what you wanted me to be, giving up myself for you."

"You never gave up yourself for me," he said quietly assured. "You became yourself."

"That shows you not only know nothing about me, you know nothing about women." She took the note from the pocket of his jeans and flattened the wrinkles out of it with the palm of her hand. "What A Woman Should Know," she read, "as if you are some kind of expert. As if you were going to write a book or something. You arrogant, sanctimonious son of a bitch."

He noticed, dully, she had actually cursed. In front of Jed.

That should have felt like he had gained a whole lot of ground with her. So why did he feel so terrible?

"Tally, you need to let me explain."

"By all means," she said. "I'll invite you to my wedding. In the receiving line you should have thirty seconds or so."

"Getting married to spite me is almost as bad as getting married because you think it's a good thing to do for Jed."

"As if I'd get married to spite you! That would mean you mattered! I'm going to marry Herbert because of the way he makes me feel. Safe. Respected. Admired. He doesn't have a list of things he'd like to change about me."

"He'd like it if you liked football," J.D. said morosely, though by now he should have figured out just to keep his mouth shut.

"Jed, come here," Tally said, throwing J.D. one last look that was solid ice, that cut him from her world.

The little boy flew into her arms. Over the ruffled surface of his son's hair, he could see she had started to cry.

"Do you want to stay with your daddy for a little while. And with Beau?" she asked, her voice broken.

Jed touched her tears, but nodded solemnly.

"Okay, sweetheart," she said and set him down, trying to smile through the tears.

"You'll only be at the Palmtree if he gets lonely, right?"

"I'm going home," she said. "I can come back and get him in twelve days or you can bring him to me."

J.D. wondered if this was the nightmare his life was going to be, seeing her for thirty seconds while he picked up his son or dropped him off.

On the other hand, maybe all was not lost. Tally *said* she didn't trust him, but wasn't she trusting him?

With what she loved most in all the world? With her child? Her nephew, the son of her heart?

Possibly this was not nearly as bad as he thought. He just had to come up with a brand-new mission strategy. That was all.

Still, as he stood at the door and watched her go, Jed standing on the porch waving uncertainly, J.D. knew he was about to take on the mission that would affect the rest of his life. There could be no mistakes this time. Not one.

He lined up Jed and Beau, and eyed them. His team. "Okay, boys," he said, "this is what we're going to do."

Tally lay on her couch, with a cold cloth over her eyes, exhausted. The drapes were closed, and despite the bright sun outside, it was dark and dreary in her apartment. The

TV was on to keep her company, but she wasn't watching the soap opera that unfolded. Her own life had become quite enough of a soap opera.

She had been crying for three days straight. The floor beside her was littered with tissues, and her cheeks were streaked and her eyes were puffy.

The phone jangled by her head, and she let it ring until she heard Kailey's voice on the answering machine.

"Tally, pick up the phone," Kailey wheedled. "There must be something I can do. And thanks for your message to buy Kleenex stocks, but I don't think that's it. Please, please, please pick up the phone."

Tally considered this, and then groped for the phone on the end table at her head. "What?" she said. Her voice sounded raspy from crying and little use.

"What are you doing?" Kailey asked conversationally.

"Getting ready to run for the Miss Canada pageant. How about you?"

"No," Kailey said, "I mean *really*."

"Okay, I'm crying, the same as I did yesterday, and the day before. I may cry for a whole week. Maybe a month. I haven't decided yet." Shades of the old control there. As if it was hers to decide how long this dark place of grief within her would last.

"This just isn't like you," Kailey said uncertainly.

Of course, no one knew the first thing about her, not even her sister. Tally had decided to give up being the strong one.

"Kailey, I am no longer engaged to Herbert and the most handsome—not to mention aggravating man—in the entire universe has played me for a fool. I have something to cry about."

"But you never cried before," Kailey said, "when all

those things would go wrong with Elana, you never fell apart.''

''I probably should have. Maybe that's what I'm doing now, making up for lost time.'' *Discovering I'm human, just like everyone else. And it sucks.*

''I'm glad you're not marrying Herbert,'' Kailey said after a long silence. ''I like him and everything, just not for you. How did he take it, anyway?''

''I don't think he's lying on his couch crying right now,'' Tally said dryly. No, there had just been no mistaking the relief in Herbert's voice, which only made everything worse, because J.D. had been right about that, too.

''You aren't crying for Herbert, either,'' Kailey pointed out, always helpful. ''You're crying because you fell madly in love with J. D. Turner, and who can blame you?''

Tally sighed. That would about wrap it up, all right. She took another tissue from the box and blew her nose, and then changed the subject. They both knew who she was crying over. She tried for a touch of humor. ''Did you buy those tissue stocks?'' Her delivery was terrible and it fell flat.

Kailey tried to go along with it, though. ''No, but I'm going to.''

''Great. Now hang up the phone. I have several boxes to get through tonight if I'm going to drive the price up.''

''I'm bringing you a pizza for supper. You don't have to let me in or anything. Just don't leave it sitting in the hall. I'll just knock and leave it for you, okay?''

Pizza sounded pretty good, actually. She'd eat it before the gallon of Double Doozy Chocolate Ice Cream that she had in the freezer. She didn't even bother to remove the spoon, just left it standing in the ice cream for stuffing convenience.

An hour later, the doorbell rang, and Tally scuffed over to the door. She had not been out of her housecoat in three days and her hair was a tangle. Her eyes were puffy from crying. No one, not even her sister, was going to see her like this. She peered out her peephole. The hallway was empty.

She slid open her apartment door and a pizza, still steaming, was on the hallway floor. It wasn't until she had leaned over to pick it up, that she saw the envelope taped carefully to the lid.

And noticed the handwriting, *Tally Smith*, masculine and spiky.

No, it couldn't be! But she was pretty sure she was never going to forget that handwriting, and pizzas didn't generally come personally addressed. She brought the pizza in and set it on her coffee table, turned the envelope over and over in her hands. Finally, she took a deep breath, and opened it up.

Inside was a single sheet of lined paper, folded.

Written across the top of it was What a Man Should Know. Whatever text there was was hidden in the fold.

"Humph," she said, and told herself to throw it away without reading it, but she was intrigued. Besides, she could read it and pretend she hadn't.

She unfolded the paper and read.

One, a man should know better than to settle for engines on the counters instead of wild, hungry nights of endless passion.

Then she noticed the photo. It had been taken in J.D.'s kitchen. Little Jed peeped out of a huge box.

She snorted again, crumpled up the paper and threw it on the floor with all her used tissues. She ate the whole pizza and most of the ice cream, then picked through the tissues to find the note and read it again.

She studied the photo. Jed looked adorable. The box was huge, like something a refrigerator came in. Sure enough, if she squinted at the picture, she could see the box was from Airbeam appliances.

So, J. D. Turner thought he could buy her forgiveness with appliances!

But he'd had them delivered to his house, not hers. Or maybe he had just found a box for Jed to play in.

Still, if he had appliances from Airbeam at his house, and he was talking about nights of hungry passion instead of clutter on his countertops, it would seem he was linking his life with hers.

Of course, she wasn't allowing it, but it was still nice to know that the great J. D. Turner wanted her.

In fact, her depression lifted, and she went and showered and did her hair. She put away the rest of the ice cream before it melted, went to bed and tried to read a book, not very successfully.

She finally phoned her sister, who had the good sense not to answer since she was so obviously party to J.D.'s scheme.

"Benedict Arnold," she said to the answering machine, and hung up. But she was smiling when she hung up.

The next morning the doorbell woke her early. She told herself to stay in bed, but after a few minutes she couldn't resist.

She went and peeked out her security hole. No one was there. But when she opened the door, a dozen red roses had been laid carefully at her doorstep. There was an envelope with them, the same handwriting announcing What a Man Should Know.

She gathered up the roses, and didn't even put them in

water before she ripped open the envelope. If anybody ever asked her she could say she dealt with the roses first.

The lined sheet of paper said: Two, a man should know that women like things that don't necessarily make sense to men. Like flowers.

An hour later the doorbell rang again, and there were more roses laid at her doorstep. She looked up and down the hall, but it was empty.

This time the note said: Lots of flowers.

And the flowers kept arriving all day, on the hour, until she had used up every vase in her house and her small apartment was filled with the aroma of roses and carnations and other flowers; the aroma of romance. She didn't even turn on one soap opera that day.

She, Tally Smith, was being romanced. Her life was not over after all. No, it seemed there was a possibility that her life was just beginning.

She showered, did her hair, put on makeup and went out for a walk early in the evening after the hourly flower deliveries had stopped. She had a salad for supper, no Double Doozy Chocolate ice cream.

The next day she was waiting when the doorbell rang, her nerves strung tense as violin strings. She actually had her eye to the peephole most of the day, not that anybody would ever know.

Even so, she missed the crucial moment when the delivery was made. The doorbell rang, while she was in the bathroom reapplying her makeup. She raced out and opened her door to find a wrapped box, the size her microwave had come in.

There was the envelope taped to the top that said What a Man Should Know.

She tore into the envelope and, Tally Smith who thought she would never smile again, smiled as she read:

Three, dog kisses are a poor substitute for the real thing. And so are these, but they'll do in a pinch.

She opened the box right there in the hallway. Thousands of foil-wrapped chocolate kisses filled the big box to the top. She took one out and unwrapped it, savored it slowly. He was right. Delicious but no substitute for the real thing.

She dragged the box into her apartment, and left it on the floor since every available surface now had flowers on it.

Tally went for a walk. It seemed to her as if the grass was the most lush shade of green she had ever seen, and the birds were singing as crazily in love with life as she had ever heard them. The sky looked bluer and everyone smiled at her.

She thought she would see him today, she was certain he would show himself, but night fell and there was no J.D. She went to bed, restless with disappointment, and dreamed dreams of his lips and eyes.

The doorbell startled her awake. She looked at her clock. Midnight. How did he get in the front security door at that hour?

She went and peeped out her peephole. Nothing. She opened the door cautiously. And there was a long, narrow beautifully wrapped box, with the now familiar envelope taped to the top of it.

She took in the box, set it on the side table and opened the envelope. The paper inside read: Four, women like getting dirty as much as men do.

She shook the box. It was light as a feather. Much too light to be old jeans and a T-shirt, perfect for a day at the mud bog. Her fingers trembling, she finally managed to open the box. In a nest of pink tissue lay a pale yellow confection as sheer and fragile as a butterfly's wing.

She took it, and shook it out. A dainty and terribly sexy negligee unfolded before her.

"Oh, my," she said, scooted into her bedroom and peeled off all her clothes. She tried it on, and stared at herself in the mirror.

"He's still trying to change you into something you aren't," she said, but the words had no bite to them. She looked glorious in the skimpy outfit. She blushed, took it off rapidly, but couldn't quite bring herself to put it away. She tucked it under her pillow where she could touch the silky gossamer folds. But she didn't sleep.

At 7:00 a.m. the next morning her doorbell rang again. She raced to it, but it was too late. The hallway was empty.

This time there was no box and no flowers, just the same heading scrawled across the envelope.

She tore open the envelope and read: Five, life needs to hold surprises. Like honeymoons. And two tickets to the Super Bowl fell out on the carpet.

She sat down right there in the hall, and stared at the tickets. Honeymoons? But they came after marriages. He hadn't even proposed yet. He hadn't—

The doorbell rang and she flung it open. Another huge box and another note. She raced down her apartment hallway in her nightgown looking for whoever had come, but they had disappeared into thin air.

She opened the note. It said: Six, men who stay single because they think they are free end up like dried-up old prunes. In brackets it said number one and number six could possibly be combined. And the box was full of dried prunes!!

She realized that was getting very close to a marriage proposal. As she was dragging the big box of prunes through to her kitchen, the doorbell rang again.

She raced back and opened it and Beauford sat there, a huge red bow tied to his collar, a letter in his mouth. She accepted the letter from him, and stepped out into the hall.

Where Beau was J.D. could not be far and she felt her heart begin to sing in anticipation of their reunion.

She hugged that dog and kissed him right on his nose. She didn't even care when his big old tongue rolled out of his mouth and caught the side of her lip. She invited the dog in, and closed the door behind him.

Standing in her entryway, she studied the envelope. It was different than the others, only in that the face of the envelope was blank. She opened it.

There was no note inside either. Just some torn up pieces of paper.

She pieced them together. She could see that once it had been a certificate proclaiming membership in the Dancer, North Dakota, Ain't Gettin' Married, No Way, Never Club.

She opened the apartment door, and called "J. D. Turner, I know you're out there. I love you madly. I'll never stop loving you. J.D., come home to me."

It was insanity. Tally Smith would never proclaim herself publicly.

Except that love had made Tally Smith a brand-new person.

The door across the hall opened, and J.D. stepped out.

"I thought you'd never ask," he said. Jed peeped out from behind his leg, and then let out a hoot and ran toward her.

"Pawtners in cwime," he announced happily, and raced across the hall to her, wrapped his sturdy arms around her legs.

"Thanks for your help, Mrs. D.," J.D. said to her

neighbor who loved the pink jogging suits, and turned and bowed to her.

Tally hugged Jed to her. She hadn't known it was possible to miss someone as much as she had missed this child. Or the big man with him.

She drank in J.D., from the sweep of his lashes, to the brand of his jeans. She drank in the breadth of his shoulders and the easy confidence of his stance. She drank in the tenderness in his eyes as he looked back at her, the softness around his mouth. She could feel her heart growing inside her chest, until it felt so full it might burst for loving him.

"He's not really a cop," Tally called to her neighbor.

"Oh, I know that by now," her neighbor said. "J.D. and I are the best of friends, aren't we, dear?"

"That we are," he said. "You have helped smooth the course of true love."

Tally's neighbor blushed and giggled and closed her door.

J.D. came slowly across the hall. Tally could not take her eyes off of him, could not drink deeply enough of the sight of him, and she noticed, delighted, he could not take his eyes off of her. He came and stood before her, touched her cheek with the back of his hand, then closed his eyes and sighed, the heartfelt sigh of a man who had found his way home.

And then he bowed his head and leaned his forehead against hers, reached out and touched Jed's shoulder with one hand.

He did not have to say a single word. Tally knew exactly what he felt for her. And she knew exactly what she felt for him.

And she felt as if she was the most fortunate woman in the whole world. A woman who had almost thrown her life away, and who had been stopped by some universal force that simply had a better plan for her.

A plan that involved love.

For without love, a life could seem full, and actually be empty. And without love, a life could be full of riches and yet the soul would feel impoverished. And without love everything could look so right, and feel so wrong.

When J.D.'s arms moved and wrapped around Tally and Jed, and he pulled them to him, she could feel his strength, and his warmth and the beat of his heart. But more, Tally could feel the sense of family that she had yearned for her whole life.

That she had tried so hard to create when she had controlled everything and everyone around her.

And that had been created for her when she had surrendered. Tally had been so afraid of losing control, but not only had she survived her loss, her feet of clay had been transformed into wings.

She had found a photograph of a man in a box, and without even knowing it, at that moment, she had surrendered to the salvation she had seen in a stranger's eyes.

"Marry me," J.D. said gruffly.

"I will," she said. And it felt like so much more than just a promise to J.D.

It felt like a promise to say yes to life, and to all its wondrous adventures.

"I will," she said to the future.

And then his lips took hers, right there in the hallway of her apartment building, and he kissed her until she was breathless and trembling.

They stepped inside the apartment and closed the door on the world, and opened it to a brand-new life.

* * * * *

If you enjoyed what you just read,
then we've got an offer you can't resist!

Take 2 bestselling
love stories FREE!
Plus get a FREE surprise gift!

✂ **Your opinion is important to us!** Please take a few moments to share your thoughts with us about your experiences with Harlequin and Silhouette books. Your comments will be very useful in ensuring that we deliver books you love to read. *Please take a few minutes to complete the questionnaire, then send it to us at the address below.*

Send your completed questionnaires to:
Harlequin/Silhouette Reader Survey, P.O. Box 9046, Buffalo, NY 14269-9046

1. As you may know, there are many different lines under the Harlequin and Silhouette brands. Each of the lines is listed below. Please check the box that most represents your reading habit for each line.

Line	Currently read this line	Do not read this line	Not sure if I read this line
Harlequin American Romance	❏	❏	❏
Harlequin Duets	❏	❏	❏
Harlequin Romance	❏	❏	❏
Harlequin Historicals	❏	❏	❏
Harlequin Superromance	❏	❏	❏
Harlequin Intrigue	❏	❏	❏
Harlequin Presents	❏	❏	❏
Harlequin Temptation	❏	❏	❏
Harlequin Blaze	❏	❏	❏
Silhouette Special Edition	❏	❏	❏
Silhouette Romance	❏	❏	❏
Silhouette Intimate Moments	❏	❏	❏
Silhouette Desire	❏	❏	❏

2. Which of the following best describes why you bought *this book?* One answer only, please.

the picture on the cover ❏   the title ❏
the author ❏   the line is one I read often ❏
part of a miniseries ❏   saw an ad in another book ❏
saw an ad in a magazine/newsletter ❏   a friend told me about it ❏
I borrowed/was given this book ❏   other: _____ ❏

3. Where did you buy *this book?* One answer only, please.

at Barnes & Noble ❏   at a grocery store ❏
at Waldenbooks ❏   at a drugstore ❏
at Borders ❏   on eHarlequin.com Web site ❏
at another bookstore ❏   from another Web site ❏
at Wal-Mart ❏   Harlequin/Silhouette Reader ❏
at Target ❏   Service/through the mail
at Kmart ❏   used books from anywhere ❏
at another department store ❏   I borrowed/was given this ❏
or mass merchandiser   book

4. On average, how many Harlequin and Silhouette books do you buy at one time?

I buy _____ books at one time ❏
I rarely buy a book ❏

MRQ403SR-1A

5. How many times per month do you shop for any *Harlequin and/or Silhouette* books?
One answer only, please.

1 or more times a week	❑	a few times per year	❑
1 to 3 times per month	❑	less often than once a year	❑
1 to 2 times every 3 months	❑	never	❑

6. When you think of your ideal heroine, which *one* statement describes her the best?
One answer only, please.

She's a woman who is strong-willed	❑	She's a desirable woman	❑
She's a woman who is needed by others	❑	She's a powerful woman	❑
She's a woman who is taken care of	❑	She's a passionate woman	❑
She's an adventurous woman	❑	She's a sensitive woman	❑

7. The following statements describe types or genres of books that you may be
interested in reading. Pick *up to 2 types* of books that you are most interested in.

I like to read about truly romantic relationships	❑
I like to read stories that are sexy romances	❑
I like to read romantic comedies	❑
I like to read a romantic mystery/suspense	❑
I like to read about romantic adventures	❑
I like to read romance stories that involve family	❑
I like to read about a romance in times or places that I have never seen	❑
Other: _____	❑

*The following questions help us to group your answers with those readers who are
similar to you. Your answers will remain confidential.*

8. Please record your year of birth below.
19 ____

9. What is your marital status?

single ❑   married ❑   common-law ❑   widowed ❑
divorced/separated ❑

10. Do you have children 18 years of age or younger currently living at home?
yes ❑   no ❑

11. Which of the following best describes your employment status?

employed full-time or part-time ❑   homemaker ❑   student ❑
retired ❑   unemployed ❑

12. Do you have access to the Internet from either home or work?
yes ❑   no ❑

13. Have you ever visited eHarlequin.com?
yes ❑   no ❑

14. What state do you live in?
_____

15. Are you a member of Harlequin/Silhouette Reader Service?
yes ❑   Account # _____   no ❑   MRQ403SR-1B

COMING NEXT MONTH

#1690 HER PREGNANT AGENDA—Linda Goodnight
Marrying the Boss's Daughter
General Counsel Grant Lawson agreed to protect
Ariana Fitzpatrick—and her unborn twins—from her custody-
seeking, two-timing ex-fiancé. But delivering the precious
babies and kissing their oh-so-beautiful mother senseless
weren't in his job description! And falling in love—well,
that *definitely* wasn't part of the agenda!

#1691 THE VISCOUNT & THE VIRGIN—Valerie Parv
The Carramer Trust
Legend claimed anyone who served the Merrisand Trust would
find true love, but the only thing Rowe Sevrin, Viscount Aragon,
found was feisty, fiery-haired temptress Kirsten Bond. How
could his reluctant assistant seem so innocent and inexperienced
and still be a mother? And why was her young son Rowe's spit-
ting image?

**#1692 THE MOST ELIGIBLE DOCTOR
—Karen Rose Smith**
Nurse Brianne Barrington had lost every person she'd ever
loved. So when she took the job with Jed Sawyer, a rugged,
capable doctor with emotional wounds of his own, she intended
to keep her distance. But Jed's tender embraces awakened a
womanly desire she'd never felt before. Could the cautious,
love-wary Brianna risk her heart again?

#1693 MARLIE'S MYSTERY MAN—Doris Rangel
Soulmates
Marlie Simms was falling for two men—sort of! One man
was romantic, sexy and funny, and the other was passionate,
determined and strong. Except they were *both* Caid Matthews—
a man whose car accident left his spirit split in two! And only
Marlie's love could make Caid a whole man again....